THE SHAME

Slave

JERROLD MUNDIS

This is for Stowe Hausner, in memory
an abolitionist of sorts

SLAVE
Jerrold Mundis
Copyright © 1967, 2012 by Jerrold Mundis
(originally published under the pseudonym Eric Corder)

Publication History
Parallax Press, New York, 1967
Pocket Books, New York 1968
Trade Paperback editon: Wolf River Press, New York, 2016
eBook edition: Wolf River Press, New York, 2012

Cover illustration: Detail from *Chatiment des Quatres Piquets dans les Colonies* (Punishment of the Four Stakes in the Colonies), by Marcel Verdier, 1849. The Menil Collection, Houston.
Cover & Interior Design: QA Productions

Books by Jerrold Mundis

Novels
(in *The Shame & Glory Saga*)
Slave Ship
Slave
The Long Tattoo
Hellbottom
Running Dogs

(Others)
Gerhardt's Children
The Retreat
Best Offer
The Dogs

Nonfiction

(For Writers)
Break Writer's Block Now!

(On Personal Money)
How to Get Out of Debt, Stay Out of Debt, and Live Prosperously
Earn What You Deserve: How to Stop Underearning and Start Thriving
Making Peace with Money
How to Create Savings (a Mini-Book)
How to Have More Money (a Mini-Book)

(General)
Teaching Kids to Act for Film and Television (with Marnie Cooper)

(Anthology)
The Dog Book

As flies to wanton boys are we to the gods,
They kill us for their sport.

—King Lear

Book 1

❧

JUD LAY MOTIONLESS ON the dirt floor. He stared at the high ceiling, blinking only after long intervals. He was listening to the grumbled angry mutterings and the occasional hoarse shouts, the sound of hammers driving nails into platforms as hasty repairs were made, infrequent horse whinnies and snorts, and a blacksmith's sledge ringing against an anvil. The market was stretching, coming to life.

Jud flexed, then relaxed, then flexed again the muscles of his right arm. The arm was asleep. Around its wrist was an iron shackle that was attached by eight links of chain to the shackle circling the left wrist of the slave beside him. Jud scratched the itching skin around the edges of the iron. His partner was awake, but neither of them spoke. No one spoke. There were only a few groans, a few coughs.

Fear crouched in the strong-walled shed: muzzle twitching, tail lashing the floor. Jud could sense it. Could smell its breath.

When you get sold in Memphis, you get sold down South. And when you get sold down South . . .

Jud wondered what it would be like to be afraid. He had been once, at least he now thought that he had, and he tried to remember it. He couldn't. He saw scenes, but the scenes evoked nothing in him save a vague and ill-defined sense of loss. His mother, Tui. Could that be right? He'd been so very small when he was sold away from her to Tiligman. The name sounded strange to his ears, Tui, but it was what had stayed with him. He remembered that she wore a bright yellow turban. And that she was very black, like darkness when the moon is behind clouds. He had never seen his father, and his father had never seen him. His mother had told him his father had been a warrior and a leader of men. They'd been stolen away, she said, from a place where there were no white men or slaves. That was hard to believe. His mother and father had been lost to each other. Jud did not know if he remembered it right or not. Or if any of it was true. Many niggers did not know who their fathers were, and sometimes they told wild stories of princes, presidents, and kings. Adoko. Osai Adoko. That was the name his mother, who was called Tui, he thought, had told him—he thought. Maybe.

He stopped trying to remember. There was so little. And it didn't mean anything anyway.

There was a grating sound as the crossbar was pulled free on the other side of the thick oak door. Then the door swung in and a man in shirtsleeves carrying a coiled bullwhip and wearing knee-high leather boots entered. From the brightness of the light that silhouetted the man, Jud reckoned it to be well past dawn. Eight, possibly eight-thirty. The buyers would be arriving soon.

"All right, nigguhs," the man shouted, "wake up! That's it,

ever' one of you. Lord Almighty, but it stinks in here. Wake up!

"Now listen, cause if'n you don', you gonna have the miseries the rest of your natural-born days. Hear? Not jus' from no whuppin' you get this afternoon, but ever' day from when your masta club you outta bed to when you drag your busted ass back to sleep. But if'n you listen, you not gonna have no miseries. No, you gonna have easy work and delights fo' the rest of your days. You gonna have warm clothes in the winter, and meat with your mush three times—maybe more—each week, and you gonna have a masta that give you no laborin' on Sunday and that ain't hardly gonna beat you at all.

"Now, any of you hankerin' to know jus' how you gonna get all this?"

There was a shifting of chains and limbs. Heads bobbed.

"Yes, Masta!" someone called, and it was as if he had pulled the lever which opened the floodgates.

The silence was drowned in a babble of voices.

The white man raised his whip. "Enuff. Enuff there. Then what you do is get them gennelmen who'll be lookin' and biddin' on you to think you the best, the soundest, and the strongest nigguh they ever did see. You don' make no trouble. You stand tall and you stand strong. You get you'self a masta who gonna pay a lot of money fo' you. Because that's the gennelman who gonna value you and treat you good.

"But if'n you don' look good and a man buy you cheap, why he gonna treat you cheap and work you like to kill you. And he gonna tear meat off you fo' no more'n scratchin' a fly outta your wool."

He flicked the whip backward and lashed out and cracked the splayed tip against a board ten feet distant, ripping away a long splinter.

"But if any of you frets me, there ain't gonna be enuff left fo' me to sell. Unnerstan'?"

They did. Very well.

They were taken out in groups of ten to be washed, greased, and auctioned off. Since the shed in which Jud was enclosed was only one of four bins of male slaves, he wasn't called until midafternoon. The day moved slowly, and the worsening tempers of the auctioneer and his assistants testified that it was a hard day. The new cotton cycle was about to begin, and planters needed good strong field hands. The bidding on likely-looking bucks was spirited. But the chief auctioneer refused to run through his prime stock in a lump. This would have lost him his best buyers. They'd make their purchases quickly and leave, and the auctioneer would have to sweat for every penny he managed to drag out of the tight-fisted men who remained. So he spaced his merchandise, refusing to offer the next group of bucks until he'd sold a group of the old or very young, those who were infirm and those who were sickly, and the females—which were not in much demand this day. The system was hard on nerves and tempers, particularly since many of the buyers had skipped lunch so as not to miss a good bargain and were uncomfortable, but prices were high, and occasionally the auctioneer could needle a man into buying an inferior slave out of sheer impatience.

As the shed emptied, those who remained grew progressively more talkative. Sometimes Jud listened to them, without any real interest, but mostly he did not. He could do simple sums, and so he occupied himself for a while by counting the number of slaves in the shed and by subtracting the number removed each time the white men came.

"I goan be sold up North," announced a slim man with yellowish eyes. "My masta goan take me up to Richman'. That in Virginy where I birthed." He lowered his voice. "A big white man goan see me there. A big white man who talk partic'lar like they does in the Bible. And he goan steal me 'way. Him an' his white fren's. They goan make me free."

"You crazy, nigguh. You been hit in the haid."

"Ain't nothin' goan make you free 'cept a grave."

"You hush that, nigguh. They hear you talk moon-crazy an' they bloody us all."

"It true," the thin man protested. "I got me a charm," he said smugly. "I paid a witchlady a whole silvuh dolla' fo' it." Around his neck was a thong. He dipped his hand beneath his shirt and held out the charm for the scrutiny of those nearest him. It was a curved, polished piece of sassafras root studded in a cabalistic design with tiny colored bead fragments.

"Lemme see." A greedy voice, a grasping hand.

The thin man thrust the charm back under his shirt. "No, suh. That my ticket to freedom. Ain't nobody touch it."

"Whut you goan do when you free?"

"Whut I goan do?"

"Yes. Whut it really mean to be free?"

The slim man scratched his head. "Well, it mean . . . it mean nobody goan whup you for nothin'."

"An' it mean you kin sleep all day if'n you want," volunteered another man.

"How you goan eat if'n you doan work?"

"Why, you gets nigguhs of yo' own, an' they does all the work."

"You git a little land," said Jud's partner, "an' you grow a little cotton an' some greeneries. You work some ever' day and you does 'zactly whut you wants with the rest of your time." He pulled against the chain that bound him to Jud. "Ain't that right?"

"I don' know," Jud said. "I'm not free. I don' know what it means." Then he closed his eyes, cushioned his head with his left arm, and thought about nothing.

The thin man and Jud were taken out in the same group. They were marched, ten of them, to the smithy. A grizzled old black man was working the smith's bellows. Jud thought about the plantation that had been his home for some sixteen cotton seasons. He didn't miss it. Nor was he glad to be gone. What he felt was for Diggs, not the plantation. Diggs, the stoop-shouldered, withered old groom with glistening black patches of skin showing through his white wool.

Diggs had taught Jud reading, and some writing. Diggs was too old to be a groom any longer. Tiligman sold him to a man who never said just what he wanted to use the old man for. Jud was sad when Diggs was sold. He was sad the same way he had been on the day he was sold away from his mother—a restless, troubled feeling.

A brief feeling.

The blacksmith was shirtless and sweaty. He had a massive gut covered with tight curls of black hair. Removing the irons was a simple process. He placed the sharp edge of a cold chisel just beneath the head of the bolt that held the manacle closed, and struck the butt a sharp blow with a hand sledge. The bolt was decapitated, and the shank was pulled loose.

"Over there," the overseer said, and pointed. "Grease up."

The area was busy with slaves preparing to appear on the block, overseers of plantation owners making ready to transport newly purchased slaves, market officials tagging slaves with the names of their masters and making change, wealthy buyers who'd bribed someone in order to get a preliminary look at the merchandise. All this was masked off from the auction block and the bidders by a high wooden fence. There were half a dozen barrels in the corner to which Jud had been sent. Around them were clustered slaves, male and female, child and adult, in various states of undress. They were smearing themselves and each other with grease.

"Strip down there," a white man said to Jud, "and git yourse'f covered. I want to see you shine, boy, ever' inch of you."

Jud removed his shirt and pants and stood naked. He dipped his hands into a barrel, came up with two great lumps of gray lard, and began spreading them across his body. The grease was cold. It was a chilly day despite the bright sun. He shivered, but he did not dislike it. He replenished his supply, working it over his legs, loins, and arms.

A white man flicked his strap across the buttocks of a girl beside Jud. She was plump but not fat, and had large conical breasts with purple nipples, and meaty thighs. Her lubricated skin sparkled.

"Come here, wench," the white man said. "I tol' you, I tol' all you niggers. You grease up good. You git out there an' *sparkle* for them gennelmen."

The girl stood before him with head bowed.

"Now whut kine of greasin' you call that, huh? You still 'bout dry as a dust storm. Whut you think, huh?"

"It whut e'er kine you say, suh. But I don' be slothful, suh, jist mayhap careless, suh."

"Well, I believes you, wench. Indeed I do. I don' opine you a troublesome nigger, so I ain't gonna hide you. But we got to git you lookin' good. You bring me two globs of that lard there."

The girl went to a barrel, scooped out grease, and returned. The white man took the lard in his hands. He applied it to her a little below her shoulders, at just the spot where her breasts began to swell out. He rubbed vigorously, warming and liquefying the lard. Then he dropped his hands over her breasts, fingers spread wide and palms cupping, massaging slowly.

"Right nice titties you got, wench, an' right perky li'l nips on 'em. Gonna make some gennelman a fine bed-warmer."

"Yes, suh." She stood motionless, expressionless.

"Lift your arms."

He worked his hands down her sides, and brought them round front again when he reached her belly. He stroked it awhile.

"Spread your legs a bit."

She planted her feet apart. He knelt in front of her, reached his arms through her legs, grasped her buttocks, and kneaded them. Then his hands went to the upper, inner parts of her thighs, slipping easily, freely over her flesh.

"Um, um," he breathed. "Yes. Um."

One hand moved up to the soft, moist juncture of her thighs and began a slow back-and-forth motion. Sweat pearls gleamed on his forehead; his eyes were nearly closed. He was rocking on his knees.

Jud had finished anointing himself. He looked at the man and at the girl with little interest. He lifted his trousers from the ground and stepped into one leg. A short white man with stumpy tobacco-yellowed teeth prodded him in the ribs.

"Not them raggy things, nigguh. Put these on. Un'il af'er you sold." He took a pair of clean and untorn pants from the several pairs he carried across one arm and handed them to Jud. Then he turned to the man and the girl. "Alworth, you'd best stop that foolery an' git these nigguhs movin'. Mista Mason be wantin' 'em on the block afore long."

"Yuh, yuh," answered Alworth. He stared at the girl's brown belly a moment and sighed. He spun her around, and slapped her on the buttocks. "Git on, nigger. Git on. Cain't tarry all day."

A second white man joined the first, and the slaves were formed into loose ranks, two abreast. The men wore only trousers, and the females were naked from the waist up, the open tops of their frocks loosely tied around their waists. The newly arrived white man walked down the line, inspecting them, while Alworth lounged off to the side, scratching his crotch and yawning.

The second white man stopped. Instead of a strap he carried a polished hickory club two feet in length and twisted with a large knot at one end. He jabbed the thin slave—the one with the yellowish eyes who'd talked about being sold up North—in the chest.

"Whut that doodad roun' your neck, nigguh?"

The slave covered the charm with his hand. "That jus' my charm, suh, jus' a li'l thing."

"Give it here. You goin' on the block clean. Don' want nobody thinkin' you a odd or contrary nigguh."

The slave took a step backward. "No, suh, please, Masta. I needs keep it with me. It doan do no harm. Please, Masta, suh!"

The white man raised his club. "Nigguh, give it here."

"Please, suh!"

"Don' mark him, Jubal," Alworth called.

Jubal lunged, ripped the charm loose, and flung it to the ground. The slave wailed. Jubal drove the end of his club into the pit of the slave's stomach. The slave doubled over, then sprawled to the dirt, eyes bulging, mouth working soundlessly.

Jubal stood back. "No marks," he said to Alworth.

RICHARD ACKERLY SHIFTED HIS weight from his right leg to his left, then back again. The inactivity, the standing, the waiting, were tiring him. And now on the block that mustee—the two-year-old baby that was almost white—was squalling hoarsely. Ackerly bounced nervously on the balls of his feet. Damn that suckler, wouldn't it ever shut up?

He could not stand crying children. The sound always cramped his stomach, made his throat tighten. *Oh, for Christ's sake, stop it,* he thought as the baby, whose mother had been taken away, wailed even louder. If he had not been hemmed in by the milling crowd of buyers he would have stalked off someplace where the sound could not reach him. It made him feel brutalized, lost; it evoked a sensation of falling through darkness, flailing out with desperate hands but never finding anything solid to grasp.

He remembered little of it now, but he had cried frequently as a baby. The clashing voices had driven him to it, hurling him into the abyss—the deep rumbling voice and the sharp stabbing one. But always he had been safely caught up from his slow and terrifying descent by soft arms, and he had been patted and crooned to for a long time after. A few times, the hands and arms that swung him up were harder and stronger, but they were warm and comforting nonetheless, and their touch was gentle. That had happened only in the beginning, though, and always they had been driven off by the sharp voice and replaced by the soft arms.

He was four years old when Amanda stormed out of the drawing room after Samuel had dismissed her shouting assault with a laugh. Richard, who had been bending with his ear to the crack of the closed doors, scampered away when he heard her coming. He wasn't quick enough, though, and she saw him and pursued him down the hall with a screech. Her blunt fingers dug into his neck. She flung him against the wall, and the breath was nearly knocked from his slightly chubby body. She stared at him, face flushed, veins prominent and throbbing, small wide-set eyes narrow, her mouth twisted in a grimace.

"*You . . .*"

She swung hard and struck him on the mouth with the back of her hand. She hit him again . . . and again . . . . She bloodied his nose, cut his lip, and bruised his face. She was breathing heavily and with each blow she gasped: "*You . . . you . . . you . . .*"

The onslaught knocked Richard to the floor. He doubled up sobbing, choking, trying to protect himself.

Then it was suddenly over and Amanda dropped down beside him. She clutched him to her, pressing his face against her small, high breasts.

"Oh!" she cried. "My baby. What has he made me do? *What has he done to you?*"

Her hands ran lovingly, desperately over his body. His face received her kisses—warm, moist kisses on his forehead, his cheeks, his lips, his throat. She surrounded him with her warmth and she rocked him back and forth whispering: "My baby . . . my little man . . . my baby . . . my little man . . ."

She held him like that for some time, and she stroked him, and she kissed him.

It happened several times again. The boy trembled whenever he heard her shrieking voice, but, after the first two incidents, he did not run away and hide, and he made only a token effort to escape when she came bursting out of a room. The punishment was painful, but also short. Not so the duration of her hands fondling him, her very soft body, and her lingering kisses.

As he grew older she stopped calling him her baby; he remained her little man, was frequently, ever more frequently, her little lover . . . .

Damn! Wouldn't that baby ever shut up? When the mustee was finally sold and removed, and new slaves were led onto the platform, Ackerly resolved to bid as high as necessary to get the two bucks that looked good to him out of this bunch. Four more, that was all he needed to round out his coffle, and then he could leave. The crowd was shifting, pressing in around him. Someone stepped on his toes, marring the high gloss to which his boots had been polished, and he grew angry.

When the bidding began, Ackerly got his first buck for seventeen hundred fifty dollars, one hundred more than he thought the slave to be worth, but that left him only three to go.

Ragged long-haired boys pushed through the crowd carrying paper cones and buckets filled with crushed ice. Bottles of flavored syrups clinked in the pockets of their baggy trousers. They argued, wheedled, cajoled, made general nuisances of themselves, and flocked to the side of any man who removed his hat and wiped sweat from his forehead with a handkerchief. Occasionally, one of them was lucky enough to sell an ice-cone for a silver coin—or, if he had to, a copper one. At intervals an excited whoop was heard from off to the side, where there was the constant click of dice from gaming tables run by flashily dressed gentlemen. Farther back was a ring of logs and on these sat rough, unshaven, sunburned men who had no money but who had come to watch the excitement. They bunched together in small groups, passed jugs to one another from which they took deep draughts, commented knowledgeably and critically on the slaves being offered, and at times bent their heads closer for the duration of a joke, erupting in laughter.

Ackerly had to wait another twenty minutes before the second buck he wanted was called. In that time a slumping, thin nigger with a desolate look was sold to a gentleman from Louisiana for six hundred dollars. The nigger became hysterical and clamored unintelligibly about Virginia and some sort of charm. At the outbreak, his new master shouted to the auctioneer that he didn't want any lunatic slave. An unshaven man in a battered slouch hat—poor white, and possibly even white trash—immediately offered the Louisianan three hundred dollars for him. This was a market vulture, a man who hovered in wait for just such an occurrence. The Louisianan accepted. The unshaven man went to claim his property, and Ackerly noted the bullwhip and the heavy leg-irons he carried. The slave would be worked to death in a matter of three or four years.

"Jud!" shouted the auctioneer.

The buck Ackerly had been eying stepped forward. He was tall, an easy two inches over six feet, and had good bones. He was dark, one of the darkest Ackerly had ever seen—a color that blended the deepest hues of blue and black.

"This here's Jud," called the auctioneer. "A Mississippi nigger from the plantation of Cap'n Aaron Tiligman. He a firs'-rate cotton hand an' got some wheelwright learnin', too. He never been whupped for nothin' worse'n daydreamin', an' he growed outen that some long time back. Ain't nobody ever take a snake to him, an' ain't the slightenest mark on his entire body.

"Now, gennelmen, I invites you to look on this 'un slow and careful. He as sound a spec'min as I seen in all my years o' sellin'. Cap'n Tiligman say he twenty years old or so, but I estimates him closer t' eighteen or nineteen. Big an' musculated as he is, he still got fillin' t' do, a lot of fillin'. Drop your pan's, boy, an' show 'em your legs an' flanks. There, jus' look on that.

"Gennelmen, this be as fine a nigger as you'll ever hope

to see. I'm settin' the minimum bid at fifteen hunnert. Now which of you gennelmen gonna offer me sixteen?"

Ackerly bought the nigger for twenty-one hundred. He was pleased. The auctioneer had not exaggerated. The buck would have brought twenty-four, twenty-five in the New Orleans market.

THE BUCKS WERE ALL of an age except one—a big gangly but promising-looking boy of thirteen or fourteen who was the younger brother of another. Young, healthy, well-made animals, twenty in all. Ackerly was conferring off to the side with two of his overseers.

Jud had little basis for comparison (only Tiligman, and Tiligman's guests), but he sensed that Ackerly's attire was of high quality. He'd never seen clothes that were made so well: a plum-colored coat with flaring tails, a string tie, not a single wrinkle on the stiff linen shirt, snug black breeches, and knee-high boots that caught and reflected the sun.

He was slim, and not much older than the slaves he'd just bought. His hair was black and lay close to his head. Long slender sideburns made his face seem even narrower than it was. He had a hooked, hawklike nose and a short mouth. He carried himself confidently and in a manner that suggested a sinewy and well-coordinated body. But when he spoke, his hands were constantly in motion, and wheeling—like frightened birds fleeing from his predator face.

Jud stood motionless, his arms hanging at his sides. He did not try to listen to his master. He did not listen to the other niggers. He listened to the sound inside his head. It wasn't really very loud, but if he listened hard he could hear it better than he could hear anything else. Once he had thought it was like the sound a field of growing grass would make, if growing grass had been able to make a sound. Then he forgot the thought. He had no reason to remember thoughts.

"Lissen here, niggers," one of the white men said.

Conversation ceased immediately. Jud listened to the man.

"This is Mista Richard Ackerly. Him and his daddy's your new mastas. You ack like civ'lize' niggers, you git treated good. You don', you git your hide torn off right down to your bone."

"I assume," said Ackerly, speaking in their general direction rather than to them, "that you all know what a working pass is, even if you've never had one. Is there anyone here who doesn't?"

There were a scuffling of bare feet and a few coughs. Finally one wary voice said, "I not 'zackly sure, Masta," and there was a general relaxing of tension among the others. Few of them knew, but they did not want to risk angering their master.

Ackerly read one of the passes. It contained the slave's name, cited the owner as Samuel Ackerly of the Ackerly Plantations in South Carolina, stated that the slave was for hire, and gave the date he was expected at the Ackerly Plantations. The pass requested that if the slave were found after that date or heading in any but a southeasterly direction before that date, he be taken into custody immediately. A reward was offered.

"The following niggers," said Ackerly, "will have these passes." He read ten names. Jud's was not among them. "You have thirty days in which to reach the plantations. Any of the five will do. If you become lost or confused, stop in any town larger than three buildings and you will be given directions.

I expect each of you to report in with at least twelve dollars. Any less, and we will assume you have stolen some."

Jud had difficulty in following Ackerly's words. His new master spoke in a way Jud had never heard before. It seemed a stiff, uncomfortable way to talk, but it was not unpleasant to hear.

"But Masta, suh," said a buck. "My ol' masta once give me a workin' pass for six month, an' they ain't no nigguh can earn more'n eight, ten dolla' a month."

Ackerly sighed and shook his head, slowly, as would one mildly troubled by an uncomprehending child. Then he nodded to one of his overseers.

The man stepped forward and slashed the slave across the face with a strap.

Ackerly was silent. He looked at the slaves with a faint— very faint—expression of amusement, then handed the passes to the overseer. The ten bucks were sent on their way. Ackerly, his men, and the remaining slaves made ready to leave.

They went first to the livery stables where Ackerly and his overseers got their mounts, and then due east out of Memphis. Ackerly rode point, and immediately behind him were the slaves, running two abreast. The overseers rode flank. The horsemen alternated between canters and trots, and the blacks had little problem keeping up with them, jogging and gaining back wind when the horsemen slowed their mounts, covering ground with long loping strides when the horses entered a slow gallop. In this way rest periods were not necessary, and the only interruptions made were to water men and animals and to fulfill natural processes.

They did not stop until the sun had sunk so low that it

appeared to be resting atop the trees on the horizon. The sound of hoofs on the hardpacked dirt and the horses' snorts brought forth the innkeeper before the white men had dismounted. He was wiping his hands on a towel.

"Cyrus," he called. "Cyrus, I say. Git on out here an' take the gennelmen's horses."

The innkeeper prepared a simple meal of stewed chicken, dumplings, and ham steaks for Ackerly and his overseers. It was good. When finished, Ackerly dabbed at his lips with the napkin the innkeeper had provided only on request. Benson, the larger of the two overseers, belched and picked his teeth with a long fingernail. Ackerly arranged to have his slaves fed—boiled rice and half a pound of bacon to be divided among them—and then went to bed.

THE MORNING STAR WAS still visible when Ackerly and his coffle left the inn and swung onto the road. The pace was brisk for the first two hours, and the exertion warmed the slaves against the predawn chill. In low spots and by creek beds there were delicate traceries of hoarfrost. These glittered with brilliant splendor when the first rays of the rising sun struck them, and disappeared within minutes.

They met horsemen on the road and an occasional gig or surrey, and a few blacks on foot or driving buckboards loaded with supplies. The whites exchanged cordial greetings as they passed, and sometimes stopped a few moments to chat. The slaves they met grinned, doffed their caps, and waved. After the sun was well on its way up the eastern sky, the pace slackened, Ackerly had his slaves sing. The cotton fields, cane fields, mills, and black work gangs of the South were redolent with song. Slaves sang as they chopped, as they hoed, as they loaded wagons, as they trooped in from the fields. And the masters loved to hear them sing, because where there is singing there is no violence, where there is singing the work is not resented and it goes faster.

The rhythmic chant, the deep baritone and bass of his slaves, wove a skein of well-being around Ackerly, making him feel that all was right in the world. Despite the agitators and rabble-rousers of the North, despite the hypocritical abolitionists who on one hand condemned Southern slavery and on the other hand condoned what (while without having the name) was in fact the enslavement of whites—whites, mind you, human beings—in the factories and dark mine tunnels of the industrial North, yes, despite these voluble fanatics, the South had held its ground.

Ackerly called a halt by a spring that bubbled up at the foot of a stand of willows. He filled his pipe and allowed his niggers to rest until he had finished his smoke and knocked the ashes out of the bowl against the heel of his boot.

There was a bronze boy named Abel among Ackerly's new slaves, slim and wiry, with outsized calves and thighs. He grew restless whenever the pace was slow, raising his knees high, shaking his arms as the slaves jogged. He was one of the lead pair and occasionally would spurt to a point just behind Ackerly's horse and mark time there until his fellows caught up with him. He ran effortlessly and seemed never to tire.

In the early afternoon, he called out to Ackerly: "Masta, kin I run on ahead? I got pow'ful juices jus' a-weepin' to be let loose, suh."

He had moved up and was trotting alongside Ackerly's horse.

"Please, suh. You kin trus' Abel. I jes' wants to do some real runnin'. I get too far up, I slow down an' wait."

Both his nigger and his horse (it had been skittish most of the morning) wanted their heads, and so after a moment's hesitation Richard said, "All right, nigger. Let's see how fast you are."

He whacked his mount's rump and drove his heels into its sides. "Gee-ah!"

The horse bolted forward and Abel was left momentarily behind. Then he was abreast of his master again, lips pulled back from his teeth in a wide smile, long legs devouring the ground. His motion was easy, fluid. Ackerly held his horse down for the first mile, seeing if the slave would tire.

But Abel showed no sign of fatigue, in fact undertook a song to show that his wind was still very much intact. Ackerly loosened his hold on the reins. The horse's long neck stretched ahead. Spittle flew back from its mouth and its hoofs pounded on the hard-packed dirt. Richard was exhilarated; he wished momentarily that his father were there, because Samuel would have enjoyed the race, and perhaps they could have enjoyed it together. Such a wish was unusual for Richard, and it soon vanished. Abel's song ceased. The boy sucked in air through his open mouth. Sweat beaded his forehead and dampened his shirt. His movements became ragged, but by the time Ackerly's horse finally did pull away, Ackerly knew that it could not sustain the pace much longer itself. Ackerly kept on until he rounded a bend and lost sight of Abel, and then stopped the horse, turned it, and went back. He found Abel still moving forward, walking briskly.

"That a good stallion," Abel said without sarcasm or arrogance. "Ain't many that kin lose me."

"You're fast," Ackerly said, and permitted himself a smile. It was good for a nigger to know he'd pleased his master. It made the nigger happy.

For the remainder of the afternoon Ackerly let the buck run on ahead whenever Abel requested. The rest of the party would find him jogging slowly—the manner in which he rested—two or three miles ahead. Or, if he had gotten too far out, he'd reverse his direction and trot back to them.

They made a brief stop in the late afternoon at an inn, ate a sparse meal, rested half an hour, and then went on. Ackerly planned on reaching Eagle's Head—the Bonestelle plantation, which was twenty miles west of Florence, Alabama—before nightfall. The Bonestelles were family friends, and Richard would be assured of a comfortable night.

They were little more than fifteen miles from the inn at which they'd eaten when a furious baying filled the heavy evening air. The road was flanked on both sides by a pine forest, heavily overgrown with underbrush. Ackerly signaled to his column to halt.

"Hounds," he said.

"Whut you figure they runnin'?" asked Benson. "Deer, or nigger?"

Ackerly listened a moment. "Nigger, I think. They're coming straight toward us."

The other overseer nodded. "An' they fer killin', not catchin'. They unleashed."

The dogs' voices drew nearer, intensified, and cracked into savage barking.

"They on his heels now," said Benson.

A black in torn clothes, with a bright line of blood staining his cheek, staggered out of the brush in front of them, fell, picked himself up, and stumbled across the road. A lean, tan-and-white blur hurtled into sight immediately after him, seemed to touch the ground once, lightly, and drove forward, and man and dog went down in a tangle of limbs.

The slave screamed. His hand rose, clutching a rock, and plunged down. The hound yelped, twisted spasmodically, and died of a crushed skull, its forelegs and hind legs extended and rigid. The rest of the pack was close at hand, singing the kill.

The fugitive teetered when he tried to stand, and then collapsed and began dragging himself toward the brush.

"He appear hamstrung," noted Benson. The other dogs burst from the woods and swarmed over the shrieking slave. The overseer asked, "Reckon we should whup them houn's off?"

Ackerly shook his head. "They don't care about this one. If they did, they wouldn't have loosed the dogs."

Ackerly's slaves gathered in a semicircle to watch, and the three white men sat loosely in their saddles, resting their hands on the pommels. There were half a dozen dogs, big rangy creatures with large flat heads. The slaughter was finished quickly and noisily.

The hounds were still ripping the carcass when a handful of armed whites strode into view. Two of them whipped the dogs back, and a single gentleman sauntered over to Ackerly.

"Good evenin', suh. Name of Church. James Church. I trust this affair did not impede your journey, nor excite your nigguhs overmuch. It's a fine-lookin' coffle."

"Thank you, suh. Richard Ackerly. You needn't worry, suh. You've caused no difficulty whatsoever."

"Good. Good. I'm pleasured there are no ladies with you."

Ackerly nodded agreement.

"I don't enjoy this in particular myself," the gentleman continued. "But what must be done, must be done. This is the third time he's run in less than a year. Wuthless nigguh. Can't cogitate what spoilt him."

"It happens sometimes. Tainted blood, I imagine."

"That's so," said the gentleman gravely. "That's so. Seems to be no other reason. Why don't you bring your bucks around and show them what happens to runners? Seems that nigguhs are growing more and more contrary every day with all the hoo-rah those fuckin'—you'll excuse me, suh—abolitionists are raisin'."

Ackerly ordered his blacks to view the corpse. It was lying face down and mutilated in a blood-drenched circle of dust. The gentleman tore away a patch of pants that covered the rump. The major part of a large branded R was still visible, though the letter was no longer complete, since one of the hounds had ripped a chunk of meat from the buttock.

Ackerly's slaves whistled and rolled their eyes.

"The first time he ran, I branded him," said the gentleman. "The second time, I snaked his back bloody, but I still gave him another chance. This time . . ."

"I have a runner," Ackerly said, "that no hound in this

country could catch. Show the gentleman your leg muscles, Abel."

The gentleman looked, more through courtesy than interest. "You don't keep him chained?"

"He's not that kind of runner, are you, Abel?"

Abel laughed and slapped his leg. "No, suh, I surely ain't."

"And why is that?" Ackerly asked.

"Where I goan run to? Who goan take care of Abel, if'n he run away? No, suh. Abel doan put one little toe where Masta doan say he should."

"You're a smart nigger, Abel. Stay that way. If you ever do run, I'll catch you and I'll cut your legs off at the knees."

Abel found this hilarious. He broke into peals of laughter. He clutched his sides.

"Yassum. Yes, suh. I believes you would, Masta. Pore Abel wouldn't have nothin' but two stumps to run on." He moved back, shaking his head and chuckling to himself.

Ackerly rested a short while longer and then started his party again. Despite their efforts, they did not reach the Bonestelle plantation until after nightfall. Ackerly was fretful and embarrassed. It was poor manners to arrive at such a late hour, unexpected.

His slaves were bedded down in the barn. He left them unchained; with the auction yesterday, any loose nigger would be picked up in a matter of hours, and there weren't any abolitionists in these parts to help them.

The Bonestelles were hospitable and friendly, and they seemed not to resent the imposition at all. They sat with him while he ate, and later in the drawing room they questioned him with sincere interest about the members of his family, and they made him relate the story of his trip in detail and give careful descriptions of the purchases he'd made. Only Mrs. Bonestelle gave any indication that their normal schedule had been interrupted. Although she flushed and apologized, she was unable to suppress a series of cavern-mouthed yawns and finally, after much apology, she and her husband went to bed, leaving Ackerly with their son, Charles.

After another brandy Charles asked, "D'you want a wench? Got a good one. Young, a yaller. She's almost a virgin. I topped her an' bust her maidenhead just last week."

"I'd be obliged."

"Shylock. Hey, Shylock," Charles called.

A tall black appeared. "Yes, suh."

"You go get Tige an' bring her to the house. Have her scrub up good an' get all the musk off herself. She's gonna spen' the night with Mista Ackerly here, an' he don't want any smelly nigger. When she's all ready, you sen' her to the big room in the north wing. You unnerstan'?"

The young gentlemen drank final brandies. Charles showed Richard to his room, and bade him good night there.

Richard undressed, hung his clothes carefully in the closet that was built out from the wall, and lay down naked upon the bed without turning back the covers. The room was warm. The fire had reduced the logs in the hearth to embers, but the embers glowed fiercely and still emanated a good deal of heat. Richard closed his eyes. He felt lazy, somnolent; it was a sensual and quasi-sexual feeling. He touched the lower part of his thighs lightly with his fingertips: short soft hairs, smooth skin. He drew his fingertips up slowly, barely touching himself, and he quivered with the sensation this produced. He stroked his belly and his hips, and a sound of pleasure slipped through his lips. He touched himself until he became aroused.

He rose up on one elbow, looked at himself, and was pleased.

There was a knock upon the door. "Come in."

The girl stepped silently into the room on bare feet, shut the door, and stood before it with her eyes cast down and her hands folded in front of her. She was barely fifteen, a quadroon of a light golden color. Her hair was dark and long and not coarse. Except for a wide mouth, her features were delicate and fine. Ackerly liked her mouth. It excited him.

"Come here," he said. "Stand at the foot of the bed."

She did so, without raising her eyes.

"Look at me. No, not just my face. Look at all of me. Yes, like that."

He rose up on his knees, facing her. And he felt indomitable, a brother of the Titans.

"Now tell me I'm the biggest you've ever seen. Tell me you're frightened."

The girl's eyebrows bunched with perplexity.

"Say it."

"You . . . you the bigges' I ever did see, Masta. I's scared of you."

"Ask me to let you go. Beg me not to hurt you."

The girl giggled.

Richard struck her with his fist. "Beg, damn you!"

There was a thread of blood at the corner of the girl's mouth. Her eyes were wide. "Please, Masta. Please, suh, doan hurt me. Please doan hurt Tige."

Richard got off the bed and walked toward her. She stepped back. "Stand still," he ordered. He walked behind her. He loosened the few hooks and eyes that held her frock closed, and then grasped her shoulders and turned her so that she faced him. He drew the frock from her shoulders. They were smooth, unblemished, honey-colored. He pressed his lips to her skin, and suddenly nipped the flesh. She stifled a little cry, but made no attempt to escape him. He lowered the frock little by little, drawing the process out, until at last the garment lay in a heap around her ankles.

Breathing heavily, he put his hands on her shoulders and forced her to her knees. He twisted one hand in her hair and yanked her head back, making her stare at his virility.

"I'm going to beat you with that. I'm going to make you cry. But I want you to love it, love it with your mouth."

He pressed her head forward and stood with his legs set wide apart, with his own head thrown back, breathing heavily through his mouth.

He stayed that way until the tremors in his legs became nearly uncontrollable. Then he thrust his hands beneath the girl's armpits, lifted her roughly, and flung her back on the bed. He threw himself atop her and stuffed a corner of the sheet into her mouth. He seized her breasts, which were not yet fully developed, dug his fingers into them, and twisted them. She writhed beneath him, throwing her head from side to side. The muscles of his forearms knotted. Tears ran from the girl's eyes. Her scream was muffled by the sheet.

When she screamed a second time, he entered her, violently.

IN THE BARN, MOST of the slaves had gone to sleep shortly after they'd eaten. One was sitting with his back to the wall,
humming softly. Two others were discussing their new master
in low tones.

"I saved now. I almos' b'lieve in God," one called Plum
said. His voice was reverent, filled with awe. "My old masta,
Mista Cook, he pore. He only own me an' my little brother,
Harris, ovuh by the stall there an' one othuh nigger. He work
us sunup to sundown an' beat us like to scramble our insides.
Din' feed us hardly nothin', an' he keep us chain' in the barn
ever' night. This the firs' time since I a striplin' that I doan
have no chain to sleep with. My old mist'ess keep sayin' I got
t' love Jesus if'n I doan wanna burn after I die. One day we
makin' soap in the yard, an' the kettle tip an' scald this other
nigger's leg. Me an' Harris jus' git a few splatters. But it scare
me, an' I pray to Jesus. An' right after, my masta come down
with lung fever. When he die, my mist'ess have to sell us. An'
now me an' Harris git ham fo' supper, and we doan have no
chain on us. Jesus hear me, 'cause it weren't no other'n him.
That certain."

Plum jabbed his finger definitively into the dirt. He had
removed his last doubts while telling the story.

"Maybe," said the other one. "Jus' maybe."

Moonlight washed in through the open space high up at
the front of the haymow. It illuminated the two speakers. On
Plum's back, Jud saw long dark wales—the ridged scars left by
a bullwhip. This was the only member of the coffle who was
obviously marked. He was strapping, broad-chested.

The other black began a story of his own. Jud spat out the
piece of straw on which he'd been chewing. He walked down

the line of stalls to the ladder that rose to the haymow, and he climbed up. The hay was thick, and his feet sank several inches as he walked across it. When he reached the opening that gave onto the pale, full-mooned night, he sat down and hung his legs over the edge.

It was quiet—as if a smothering blanket lay over the countryside. Jud liked the stillness. He looked up at the stars. They were very far away; that was all he knew about them. Or had ever wanted to know. He was aware of a huge, empty distance that lay between him and them. Very often when it was still like this and when he was looking at the stars, he felt as if his body were something like a tightly lidded kettle. There was pressure within him, just as there was the pressure of steam in such a kettle suspended over the fire. If he were somehow to be punctured at a moment like this, he thought that whatever was inside him would rush out with a loud hiss, rise toward the stars, seek the emptiness, and dissipate itself.

He did not know whether or not he liked this feeling. But he returned to it again and again.

There was a sharp whirring of wings as a bat, driving blindly toward the barn, sensed an obstacle in its course and veered straight up.

Jud worked a nail free from the weathered, semi-rotten wood. He scratched a diagonal line into a board. Then he bisected this with a second line. He became engrossed in the task, and when—quite some time later—he finished, the board was marked with an intricate and tightly circumscribed design of no particular significance.

He lay back in the hay and cupped his hands beneath his head. Though there were no impediments to escape, the thought of running did not occur to him. Why should it? And if it had, and he fled, where would he run to? What would he do when he arrived?

A horse snorted below, and loose boards clattered. A sleeping slave grunted and rolled over. The horse whinnied this time, a shrill and louder sound, and again the boards clattered.

"What goan on there?" asked a dull voice.

A few sleep-muttered imprecations arose from the stalls.

Then a clear, strong voice said, "Oh-um! Um! Look at that, hey. Hey, look. He tryin' t' top that ol' mare. He think he a rutty stallion! Hey, rise up. Look here."

Jud yawned, stretched, and closed his eyes.

"Oooh-eee, boy! Masta catch you, he cut you sure. Make a wench out'n you."

"You think that a wench?"

A boy giggled. "Ain't never had a wench. Weren't none where I lived. Jus' Masta, Masta's son, and some bucks. Masta's son do this all the time."

Jud fell asleep.

THE LEAVETAKING WAS BRIEF and good. The Bonestelles were truly a refined and hospitable family, and Richard was tempted to pass another day or two with them. His father, though, would be impatient to see the new blacks. Also, there was the consideration of weather. It was holding nicely, but the early spring rains were due, in fact even late this year, and Richard wished to take advantage of each good traveling day. But paramount was the fact that he was an unexpected guest. Decorum would not allow him to stay.

They made good time, covering sixty to seventy miles each day. Once storm clouds moved in from the north in the early morning, darkened the sky, and rumbled angrily through the day, but eventually drifted south without relinquishing any of their moisture. The coffle left Alabama and moved through Georgia. The white men were pleased; they made jokes and laughed as they neared the South Carolina border. The slaves could discern nothing that differentiated one state from another, but shared the enthusiasm of their masters.

Ackerly gave Abel permission to run ahead whenever the boy desired. As often as not the coffle moved without Abel, but never was he absent for more than an hour at a time. Near the South Carolina border the blacks sensed a growing uneasiness in the white men: Abel had been gone for an hour and a half.

The white men urged their horses into a slow gallop and the tired slaves strained to maintain the pace. The running line became ragged. The overseers used their straps. At a bend on the top of a hill, bordered by dogwood trees, Ackerly pulled hard on the reins and brought his mount to an abrupt, stamping halt. An open-topped surrey stood in the center of the road. A stout man with a florid face sat in the rear seat alongside a wispy woman who was fanning herself. An elderly black in red livery held the reins of a matched pair of gray geldings.

Abel was lying at the edge of the road, blood pulsing in clots from his mouth.

The liveried black assisted his master down from the surrey. The gentleman waddled over to Ackerly as Ackerly dismounted.

"It's nigh time you arrived, suh, nigh time. I presume this is your nigguh." The fat man gestured vaguely in Abel's direction.

"Yes, suh. He is." Richard walked toward Abel.

The stranger broke into a kind of rolling trot in order to match the younger man's long strides. "What kind of idiocy prompts you to let a nigguh run loose like that?"

Richard stopped, turned, and stared at the man. The man backed two steps away. Richard turned to Abel again.

The little man puffed out his chest. "You could of killed my wife and me. Do you know that? This crazy nigguh ran right around the bend smack into my horses. They trampled him and dragged the surrey over him. If my boy wasn't quick, my wife and I'd be laying in the road, too."

Richard knelt on a knee beside Abel. His overseers came to his side, and behind them—carefully, so as not to crowd too close to the whites—the slaves bunched up.

"Does your daddy know you let his nigguhs run free?"

Richard snapped his head up. "Does *your* daddy approve of your running down other people's property?"

The Georgian's red face deepened in hue. He *harrumphed* in his throat and muttered, "Impertinent striplin'."

"Where does it hurt, boy?" Richard was not sure whether Abel was even conscious.

Abel's lids opened. Pain furrowed the skin around the eyes. His jaw moved, but the only sound that escaped him was a wet grunt. Then he was racked by blood-spraying coughs.

"His lungs are punctured," Richard said, drawing back some. Then he said, "Move your legs, boy. Go on, just a little bit."

Abel gritted his teeth. The effort cabled the muscles in his neck. Then he sighed, a bubbling sound, and tears rolled from his eyes. "Ah caint," he managed to whisper.

Richard stood. "His back is broken," he said to the Georgian. "That's a sixteen-hundred-dollar buck you've ruined. I expect full payment. I'll make out a bill of sale for you."

"What! You expect me to pay you sixteen hundred for a near-dead nigguh?"

"I'd be pleased to go to the local sheriff with you, if you don't think you're responsible."

They moved away from Abel to settle the matter.

Abel rolled his eyes, scanning the ring of expressionless faces above him. The overseers left first. One by one the slaves followed, until only Jud was left with Abel. He squatted down. Abel's face had a fascination for him that he did not understand. He'd seen men who were dying and who were afraid of dying. There was some of that in Abel's face, yes, but there was something else, too. He didn't know what it was. Abel looked at him quietly, and Jud peered back intently into his face, trying to trap the elusive thing.

They stayed that way for several minutes. Then, weary, Jud rose. Abel made a sound. Jud hesitated; then he lowered himself again. Abel's lips moved, and Jud leaned forward. When he was very near, Abel grasped his hand. It was a feeble hold, and Jud could have freed himself easily. But he didn't. Instead, he looked down at both their hands; then he stared at Abel's face again. Abel lost consciousness a few moments later. Jud got up. He walked away from the boy.

Richard and the Georgian had resolved the issue. The Georgian looked angry.

"Is he still alive?" Richard asked Jud.

"I don' know."

"Well, go see."

Jud felt a heartbeat when he placed his hand on Abel's chest. He nodded to Ackerly.

"What do you want done with him?" Richard asked the Georgian.

"Oh—" the Georgian waved a pudgy hand, "put him on the back of the surrey. Tie him with the trunk straps."

Richard shrugged. He pointed to Jud and to another slave. "You and you. Strap him to the backboard."

Abel groaned but did not regain consciousness when he was fastened to the back of the surrey, hanging slightly away from the backboard and held a few feet above the ground by straps around his chest, his waist, and his legs. His arms dangled free. His fingertips nearly brushed the dirt.

Ackerly and his party went back with the Georgian to his plantation, which was only a few miles distant. When they arrived at the whitewashed log-and-mortar Great House, Abel was dead.

Ackerly entered the house with the planter to make out a bill of sale and to receive his money.

Jud studied Abel a few moments. Then he turned to stare at the featureless wall of the house.

He listened inside his head to the sound of growing grass.

THE PORTAL UNDER WHICH they passed was formed of two massive marble columns and a marble pediment. The plantation's name—OLYMPUS—was set into the pediment in stylized Gothic script of black wrought iron. The road—as opposed to the public road, which was dirt—was layered with two inches of white gravel; no visitor to the Ackerly Great House would have to contend with dust or mud.

Richard whooped and kicked his mount. The horse galloped forward, spraying the slaves with tiny bits of gravel, and was soon out of sight. The slaves trotted after him, bare feet padding over the stone. For a short while they moved beneath the bare interlocking branches of stately oaks that towered on either side; then they left the cover of the trees, and a low murmur swept their ranks.

Plum, the boy with the scarred back who'd spoken of his deliverance by Jesus, grabbed his little brother's hand and cried out: "Oh, Lord! We saved, I tol' you we saved, Harris. It beautiful as heaven."

It was not beautiful, but it was the skeleton of beauty, and Plum saw the fulfillment of what it promised. A huge three-story Great House a quarter-mile away dominated the landscape. There was a great rolling lawn that reached from the edge of the oaks to the house. The grass was brown and dry now, but after the rains it would grow lush and green. There was a profusion of leafless willow trees, magnolias, and dogwoods. There were graveled walks. White wooden latticeworks shone brightly in the sun; soon the rain and sun would infuse life into the vines that twisted around them. There were orchards too small to be practical, solely for decoration. There were terraced flower beds. There were . . .

The eye was assaulted by latent opulence, too much to be assimilated at first sight. Several figures were standing in the portico when the two overseers brought the slaves to a halt before the building. Richard was flanked on one side by a stocky, middle-aged man of medium height, and on the other by a dour woman with small, wide-set eyes. There were two other white men, guests; one puffing on a clay pipe, the other wearing a cleric's collar. A handful of liveried house servants had come out to see the new slaves.

Richard took his father's arm and led him eagerly to examine the new property. Samuel Ackerly listened attentively as his son described each slave's particular merits and skills. The older man prodded and poked with practiced fingers, felt muscles, and examined teeth, ears, and eyes. He mumbled to himself, affirming what Richard had said; he noted that Plum's left eye was a trifle rheumy and should be rinsed. Richard hovered at his side. Samuel was several inches shorter than Richard. His hair was pepper gray and had receded far up his forehead. His face was full, but not jowly. A short thick neck was set upon massive shoulders, and from those shoulders depended heavy and disproportionately long arms. His chest was expansive. He looked as if he had been constructed of heavy metals that had been reduced to their most elemental properties and compressed into an ingot of astonishing density.

"Well," Richard said when Samuel was finished, "what do you think of them?"

Samuel stroked his bristly jaw. "I—"

"They're lovely, dear." Amanda Ackerly swept from the portico to her son's side with a rustle of her green silk dress. "You have a fine eye for niggers, and your mother is proud of you."

She spoke slowly and with a more obvious attempt at precision than did her husband or her son. Though she was a

Lockwood—a New Orleans Lockwood—and had had a pampered and luxurious childhood, she had not been educated by English tutors as had the Ackerlys, and except in moments of high stress she constantly strove to avoid the more degenerate speech patterns of the South.

"Sound," Samuel said. "They all seem sound."

"They are *excellent* animals, Richard. Your judgment is impeccable."

Samuel pointed to Jud. "How much did you say you paid for him?"

"Twenty-one hundred."

"High, too high. I didn't want you to go over two thousand."

"He's worth much more than what you paid for him, dear," said Amanda to her son.

Samuel dismissed the slaves, telling Benson to have them scrubbed down and issued new pants and shirts.

Amanda took the guests into the drawing room, and Samuel and Richard retired to the study to go over the details of the purchases. Richard idly trimmed a hangnail with a silver clasp knife as Samuel made entries in his books. Richard respected his father's power—for Samuel Ackerly was a powerful man—but otherwise thought him a boor. Samuel had been born to money and position, but only the repeated hammering of the years had broken him to gentility, and even then not completely.

Richard looked at his father, who was sucking his cheek as he worked, and sneered inwardly. By what right had Samuel criticized the price he had paid for that coal-black nigger, the one whose silence Richard was beginning to interpret as a kind of quiet insolence? He would like to see his father come home with a better bargain. Richard felt his ears redden. If he objected to the price, he could have said so in private, couldn't he? It wasn't necessary to mention it in front of the guests, and more mortifying, the house niggers. To say nothing of the new bucks themselves. Particularly that Jud. He thought about the big black. His anger flared.

WHEN THE RAINS CAME, they came in abundance. Large splattering drops fell continuously for four days. The paths between the shanties that housed the plantation's more than two hundred slaves were ankle-deep with mud. After the first downpour came a week of intermittent storms and showers, and only infrequently did sunlight penetrate the gray-black clouds that lay heavily across the sky.

Jud was busy during the rains. There were hoes and choppers, axes, spades, and hatchets to be fitted with new shafts. There were surrey and buckboard wheels to be repaired, new axles to shape, hubs to bore. The carpentry shop was well equipped and the wood was seasoned and of good quality. He enjoyed the activity and worked hard, much preferring the shaping of wood to the monotony of the cotton fields. Actually, the difference rested not so much in the nature of the work as in the fact that he could be alone while he did it. He liked that.

His foot was working the pedal that operated a lathe, and he was moving the sharp blade of a shaping tool down the revolving length of a new spoke. The door opened, was caught by the wind, and banged against the wall. Samuel Ackerly stomped in, muddying the floor. He took his dripping slouch hat from his head, slapped it against his mackintosh, and wiped some of the larger drops of water from his face with his hand. He closed the door.

Jud continued with his work. He'd noted that his new master wandered through the work areas incessantly, and that the mere fact of his presence signified nothing in itself. As often as not, Samuel would depart without a word, and sometimes without examining a single thing, having come for no reason that Jud or anyone else could discern.

Samuel scratched the bald spot on the crown of his head and muttered to himself. He walked to the wall and checked a sheaf of hoes that Jud had fitted with new handles. He nodded.

"Yes. Mm-hm. Yes. All right." Then he singled one out. "No, no good at all. Here, you. Look at this blade. It's cracked. Yes, I know, just a small crack, but it means that the metal is inferior. I don't want any faulty equipment on Olympus. Save the handle, but throw the blade out."

He freed the spoke on which Jud was working from its clamps, held it up, and scrutinized it.

"A fine piece of work. Nicely done. Yes." He set the spoke down and put his hat back on. "After supper I want you to go to the wenching shed. You spend the night there with Clea. Get a good strong buck from her and when it's born, you can spend the day idle. Fishing, lying in the sun, whatever you want."

"Yes, suh."

Ackerly left. Jud replaced the spoke, pumped the foot pedal, and picked up a concave piece of stone. The spoke had been shaped; it needed only to be smoothed now. He applied the stone to the spinning wood and began to grind down the roughness.

The wenching shed tonight. All right. Where he slept made no difference to Jud.

From the carpentry shop, Samuel went to the stable, where he stayed for a while watching a couple of his blacks pitch hay down from the loft. Later, he stood out in the rain, discussing something with himself.

It was already dark by the time the supper kettle was brought around to the shanties. Cornmeal mush was ladled onto Jud's tin plate from a huge iron kettle. He was also given a piece of boiled fat meat. One of the shanty's tin spoons had been broken. Jud was the newest of the four slaves who lived in the single room, so he ate with his fingers. While he prepared to go to the wenching shed, the other three bucks made jokes—anatomical jokes, envious jokes. Clea was pretty.

Jud grinned. Facial expressions were useful. They made other people think you understood them, were one of them. Jud had learned this early; he had practiced before a broken piece of mirror on Tiligman's plantation. He could portray half a dozen convincing responses, which were more than enough for any nigger.

The wenching shed was a long and low structure partitioned into four cubicles. Weak, dirty yellow light seeped through the cracks of three doors. He tried the first. The couple within interrupted their activities only long enough to give him a brief glance. He tried the second and he found Clea.

She was lying naked on her back, gripping her ankle, leg weirdly bent, and gnawing at the nail on her big toe. She released her ankle when he entered, and she spat something from her mouth and smiled. One tooth was black—dead. She was pretty. A "yaller" of perhaps sixteen years. She had a high forehead, large round breasts, and a fine network of white stretch-scars around her belly testifying that she'd borne at least one suckler.

"Doan jus' stan' there," she said. "Git in, git in." She threw her head back and laughed. Her breasts jiggled. "Jesus! They sen' me a nigger who doan know no better'n to come outta the rain. Close that door. It a cold wind a-blowin'. Lemme see you, nigger. Um-*mm*. You big an' black. I reckon you about the most black nigger I ever did see. You big all over? Shuck down an' lemme see."

Jud walked to the foot of the bed. It was a narrow plank bed. There was a layer of cornhusks on the planks and over these had been thrown a rough woolen blanket. On the wall was a small shelf which contained a clay saucer filled with crude oil. A piece of rag was burning and sputtering in the saucer, providing unstable light and giving off ribbons of black smoke. Jud removed his clothes and dropped them on the floor.

"Big enough," the girl said, mostly to herself. "But not too big for Clea. Masta Richard, he git me with a wench suckler las' year, an' Masta Richard ain't hardly bigger'n a li'l chile there. You goan git me knocked with a big muscley buck, I 'spec.'"

Jud said nothing.

"Hey, what the matter with you, nigger? Why you look at me like that? You funny in the head—or jus' dumb?"

Jud smiled, and hoped it was a friendly smile.

"Tha's better. You come here next to Clea an' sit down. We can't do nothin', lessen you git yourself inneres'ed. Look."

She cupped a breast and flipped the nipple with her finger.

"You like that? You try it. Um. Um. Yas." She stroked him. "Now you startin' to be alive. I thought you was a dead nigger."

Jud followed the lead of his sex. There seemed to be only the remotest connection between him and what he was doing. He remembered dimly something that had happened when he was very young with a dark little girl on Tiligman's. Reaching, reaching with the moving creature beneath him, he felt the memory straining to clear itself in his mind; then it disintegrated violently and he became one with his act for a brief, intense moment. He gasped. It was gone. Everything was gone.

Nothing had ever been.

His head ached.

Clea sighed, relaxed the pressure of her arms around him, and closed her eyes.

Jud listened to the sound inside his head.

THE SOUND OF THE rain, growing lighter now, was what Richard listened to in the darkness of his room. And the sound of his father's rumbling laughter, which occasionally rolled out of the drawing room and found its way up the staircase and drifted down the halls of the second story. Richard had excused himself an hour ago from the company of his parents and the two guests, Reverend Hartwell and Major Delmore. As far as Richard could determine, they were still arguing—no, three of them were arguing. The fourth, his father, merely smiled and sat like some impregnable fortress, offering nothing constructive of his own, shaking his head and forcing the others to storm his walls, now and then firing brutal and powerful cannonades at them. Richard had been on the verge of shouting, but a single slashing glance from his mother had silenced him. One does not shout at one's father in the presence of guests. Richard's stomach had been rippled by spasms of nausea. He had gone to bed.

He was feverish. He rubbed his hips. He rubbed his thighs. He wanted a wench, one like he'd had at the Bonestelles'. Damn that minister! Damn propriety! Well, Hartwell and Delmore would be leaving tomorrow. But that didn't help tonight. He squeezed his hands into tight fists. His nails dug into his palms. His forehead was damp. There was a tightening and cramping between his legs. Oh, Christ! Christ. The rain pit-patted against the window. The air was stuffy; it was hard to breathe.

Like it had been in the barn. He could see the bales of hay he had stacked around himself, above himself, leaving only a small opening for air and light. Fifteen years ago. No, he was twenty-four now. Sixteen years ago. Fifteen? What difference? What difference! He was alone, high up in the loft, sweaty, lungs oppressed by the thick sweet smell of the hay. He was on his knees. Oh, the pressure between his legs! The damning, sweet, horrid straining. It wouldn't stop. He didn't want it to stop. Oh, stop it, yes. It was destroying him. No, no. More. More! His bloodied hands shook so badly that he could hardly hold the knife. The mutilated, furry little thing that had been a puppy was spread-eagled on the straw. It no longer struggled, only shuddered. It was dying. It was ending. Not yet, a little while longer. Please . . .

He fell asleep, and he thrashed on the bed, became entangled in the blankets, struggled with his pillow. He dreamed he was in the loft of the barn, and his bloodied hands were trembling and the mutilated body of his mother was . . . He woke up with a little cry. He ground his knuckles into his eye sockets and gasped air. A dream. About what? What? He couldn't remember. He wanted a woman. He wanted to crush her.

IN EACH CORNER OF the drawing room was a standing flambeau imported from Rome. The candles eliminated the shadow that might have been thrown by those smaller but more numerous candles on the crystal chandelier that hung from the center of the high ceiling.

Reverend Hartwell formed a triangle with his hands and rested his chin upon its apex. "Then there are those of my calling who believe that our Lord has set aside a section of heaven specifically for the souls of niggers."

"Perhaps," said Samuel, "he visits them there in blackface."

"Samuel!" said Amanda. "Your vulgarity is not appreciated."

Samuel looked abashed. "Well, it doesn't seem too illogical that if niggers do have souls and if God has ceded a part of heaven to them, then he might very well manifest himself to them in a guise they could comprehend. Isn't that possible, sir?"

The minister flicked his tongue over his lips and eyed Samuel with distrust. He cleared his throat. "Ah, well . . . ah, yes. The, ah, labyrinths of higher theology and metaphysics are indeed, ah, complicated and in large part still, ah, uncharted, one might say. It is possible, *possible* I say, that—ah—granting the first premise, then our Merciful Father might, *might,* reveal his sacred being to them in a familiar . . . that is, as you say, a form they could comprehend." He dabbed his forehead with his handkerchief.

"I see," said Samuel. "And if horses have souls and if God has set apart a corner of heaven for them, then it follows that he might appear to them in the form of, say, a giant stallion."

Amanda sprang to her feet, scarlet. "You . . . You . . . !"

Samuel rose with deliberate slowness. The major was packing his clay pipe. Reverend Hartwell was studiously wiping his glasses.

Samuel smiled and inclined his head. "You'll excuse me," he said, and left the room.

Amanda sat back down. She stared into space, lips drawn into a thin bloodless line.

Major Delmore lighted his pipe and puffed noisily. Reverend Hartwell returned his pince-nez glasses to his nose. There was a moment's silence.

The minister leaned forward and in a low and solicitous voice said, "You poor, dear woman."

Amanda demurred with a brushing motion of her hand. She said brightly, "Reverend, what are your own beliefs concerning the nature of niggers?"

It was a brave thing, she thought, possibly heroic. She knew that her guests admired her fortitude.

The reverend observed another moment of silence to demonstrate that he truly did understand and sympathize with her situation. Then he said, "Rather orthodox, my dear.

The nigger is a beast created with articulate speech, and hands, so that he may be of service to his master—the White Man." These words flowed with practiced ease. "Further, he is not simply *a* beast, but *the* Beast, to which the Holy Scriptures make so many references. He is the highest order of apes, and . . ."

SAMUEL WAS HATLESS. A light rain fell on his unprotected head. It was stopping. It would be clear by morning. He left the gravel path and headed around the house toward the shanties. He wanted to stalk through the mud, to get his feet dirty. The major—clamoring "The South! The South!"—was an idiot. But he did have a point: if that bearded scarecrow Lincoln *did* get the nomination . . .

But that fop-faced, empty-headed preacher. Balls, what a moron. Of course, niggers had no souls. For that matter, Samuel wasn't sure he had one himself. But it was all irrelevant. If God was sitting up there somewhere, no one was going to budge him one way or the other, so . . .

"God, souls, niggers, war, the Union. Ach!" Samuel spat.

He stopped, breathed deeply, and sighed. It wasn't Hartwell, and it wasn't Delmore. It was Amanda.

Time was when she couldn't reach him. Time was when her sniping attacks rolled off him like rain off a mackintosh. He was growing old, he imagined, and weary. Chinks were beginning to show in his armor, and Amanda thrust her talons with unerring accuracy into each of these crevices. He had married her six weeks after he'd met her on Shrove Tuesday in Mobile. She was sharp-tongued during their courtship, but he found that appealing; it showed spirit and strength. She soured—or maybe came into her true nature—the instant she saw Olympus. She thought its munificence was being flaunted at her. She thought Samuel's praise of her own lineage and family wealth was simply condescension. She resolved, as she stepped from the carriage, to make herself ruler of Olympus—and ruler of the man who owned it. She did not. And the fact that she did not served only to drive her to further extremes.

She took his son away, but since he had never *had* his son, she hadn't really taken anything of value from him.

But Samuel was growing old. Much older, he thought, than his years. He was slowly being ground to dust.

The sky was clearing; a few stars were visible. It was a big sky, immense, awesome, overwhelming.

He strode quickly to the nearest shanty. He pounded on the door until it opened. A frightened black face peered at him through the crack between door and frame, and then swung the door open wide.

"Git up. Git up!" the slave cried to his fellows. "It Masta Samuel come to us. Git up. Strike a light there."

There was a quick shambling. Flint and steel sparked. The oil lamp sprang to life. Four blacks huddled near the fireplace, apprehension freezing their faces.

Samuel closed the door behind him, kicked some litter from the floor, and sat down with his back to the wall.

"Niggers," he said, "talk to me."

A RAINBOW ARCHED ACROSS the sky at dawn, lingered an hour, then faded, leaving the heavens an unmarred, deep blue. Small, puffy white clouds edged in from the east. It was Sunday. The slaves had no chores.

Reverend Hartwell's service began at eight forty-five. Less than half the slaves could have crammed themselves into the meeting shed, and since the day was clear, the address was given out of doors. Olympus's black population sat in the mud. Cleaning their clothes later would consume a large part of their day. The minister stood upon a wooden platform. On his right sat Amanda and Samuel. Richard and Major Delmore were seated on his left.

The voice of God's emissary was stentorian now that he was in his milieu. He demanded, he implored, he entreated, he exhorted. As God was the white man's master, so was the white man the nigger's master; and as God demanded obedience and homage from his servants, so did God expect niggers to give homage and obedience to their masters. God was this, God was that . . . . It went on for more than an hour and a half.

The blacks were happy. The preacher was an excellent performer, and they always enjoyed a good show.

When the minister spoke of God's mercy, Plum leaped to his feet and gave testimony of his own deliverance, praising the Father, Son, and Holy Ghost. Reverend Hartwell was delighted.

Few of the slaves believed in God, but it made their masters happy to think they did. And the happier the master, the better off the slave. So they clapped their hands, stamped their feet, rolled their eyes, and shouted *Amen*—and they found that they had a good time doing it, so in the end they supposed it was a better thing to have a God than not to have one.

Amen!

And every time a preacher visited the plantation, they had bacon and salted herring with their mush and pone, and Billy Seldoms—biscuits made with shortening.

AMEN!

While the minister harangued them, Jud stared at the hair of the girl sitting in front of him. It was long and lustrous, black as ink, tightly waved rather than coiled. Individual strands caught the sun as she moved, sparkling. He thought that if he touched it, it would be as soft as the filaments in a milkweed pod.

The meeting ended with a hymn led by Reverend Hartwell, who swung his arms vigorously. The slaves made their way back to their shanties. Jud walked behind the girl. He had glimpsed her briefly when she had arrived yesterday in a buckboard. She'd been purchased in Richmond with a hand-ful of other females. Virginia was the birthplace of American slavery, and its wenches were considered to be of the highest quality.

She walked alone, head high. Her neck was long and slim, her skin copper. She was young, barely nubile. Her body was still somewhat gangly, but had begun to fill out.

"You, girl. You, Delia."

The girl stopped and turned.

"You wait there." An old crone behind Jud clutched the arm of a younger slave and hobbled through the mud as best she could.

Jud stopped. He faced the girl. Her forehead was high and

smooth. Her eyes were narrow and the pupils were as black as her hair. Her nose was straight and thin—the legacy of white blood. Her lips were wide. There was a small cleft in her chin.

She did not acknowledge Jud's presence. The granny came abreast of them and clawed for a grip on Delia's arm.

"You come wif me," she rasped. "No sloth today. I needs wenches to make field pants, an' you a sewer."

Delia let herself be taken away, but even with the old woman's fingers curled about her arm, it seemed as if the girl were doing precisely what she wanted to.

Jud and a younger buck who shared the shanty worked on the building's roof until late in the afternoon. The rains had revealed several leaks. They ripped out weather-rotted planks and replaced them with new, rough boards, fastening them to the rafters with wooden pegs.

Richard Ackerly, checking the plantation's activity from horseback, drew his mount up and ordered Jud down from the roof.

"My father says you're a good nigger, one of the best wheelwrights we've ever had." He studied his cuticles. "He takes a great deal of pride in you. As if he'd had his eye on you, and acquired you in a shrewd round of trading. He's evidently chosen to forget what he said to me the day I brought you home. What do you think of that, nigger?"

"I don' know, Masta."

Richard laughed. "No, of course you don't. Incidentally, who gave you permission to use nails instead of pegs on that roof?"

Jud spoke carefully. "They all pegs, suh. I made 'em myself at—"

Ackerly's leg shot forward and the toe of his boot sank into the pit of Jud's stomach. Jud grunted, dropping to his knees and one hand.

"I asked you a question, nigger."

Jud pushed himself up.

"The next time I pass by, I don't want to see a single nail. Just pegs, and nothing else. Is that clear?"

"Yes, suh." Jud looked into Richard's eyes. "I unnerstan'. I unnerstan' perfec'ly."

Richard smiled. "Yes. I think you do."

He kicked his horse and rode down the avenue between two rows of shanties. Niggers scrambled out of his way.

Jud climbed back up to the roof. There was a bucket of warm pitch there, ready to be spread. He sat down and stirred the thick gum with a brush for a long, thoughtful while. Then he began to seal the seams.

TWO DAYS OF HOT sun burned the excess moisture from the earth, and the plowing began on Tuesday morning. Jud worked with a team of oxen in the north quadrant. Ten other team drivers worked with him in this area. They threw the dirt into six-inch beds by turning furrows both ways toward a given center. The teams and drivers in this quadrant were under the supervision of Chaskey—a bull-necked black foreman with a sprinkling of gray in his wool.

During the early part of the morning, Richard Ackerly rode into Jud's quadrant, conferred with Chaskey, and rode away. After Richard's visit, Chaskey became more overbearing than usual, driving the slaves hard, laying on the leather strap. One man working a team of mules lost his temper and swore at the foreman. Chaskey whipped him furiously.

Jud felt the bite of the strap several times, but said nothing. The tracings were looped about his neck. He was shirtless. Sweat ran down his back in rivulets and dampened his pants. The wooden handles of the plow sluffed skin from the large calluses on his hands.

Women and children brought them their midday meal only after the sun was well past the meridian. They had water—but not much and not too cold; sunstroke was always a danger in the fields—a few ounces of pone, and dried apricots to suck and chew.

They went back to plowing. Chaskey spent a good deal of time near Jud. He criticized frequently, using the strap to emphasize his words. The blade of the plow struck a huge stone beneath the soil. Jud jerked the tracings hard, and pushed up on the handles trying to jump the blade over the rock.

"Whoa, there. Whoa!"

But the blade caught, and the oxen lumbered dumbly ahead a few steps before they stopped. There was a wrenching sound and a long lateral split appeared in the wood where it fitted into the iron socket. Chaskey was there in an instant.

"I'm gonna have to bring 'er in," Jud said. "It need fittin' with new wood."

"Lazy goddamn nigger." Chaskey swung the strap. "You wreck that thinkin' you won't haf to work no more, din' you?"

Chaskey whipped Jud across the face. Jud stepped back and raised his hand. Chaskey pressed in, working the strap past Jud's guard.

"Don' do that, Chaskey. Not on my face. You tear out my eyes."

"Whut you goan do, nigger? Show me what you goan do." Chaskey's attack grew more violent.

The skin of Jud's face was hot and tight. His right eyelid was puffing out, obscuring his vision.

"Come on, nigger. Do somethin'." The strap hissed through the air, cutting into Jud's face.

"Chaskey—"

"Stop me, nigger. Stop me. I goan blind you sure."

Jud reached and clamped his fingers around Chaskey's wrist. He twisted slowly, steadily, to the side. Chaskey resisted—without effect. The strap dropped to the ground, and Jud released his hold.

"Not my face," Jud said. "You hurt me bad that way."

Chaskey dropped into a crouch. "You know whut you jus' done?" he rumbled.

"I bring this plow in now."

Chaskey wrapped Jud in a bear hug, positioned his head under Jud's chin, and began to force Jud's head back. The bones in Jud's spine strained.

"Don', Chaskey. Lemme loose."

Chaskey grunted and increased the pressure.

The other slaves ran from their teams to watch.

"Chaskey . . ."

Jud was short of breath. There were pains in his back and at the base of his neck. He pushed himself backward and pivoted to the side simultaneously. When they crashed to the earth, Jud was atop Chaskey. The impact broke the foreman's hold. Jud pulled free, and both men gained their feet.

Chaskey lunged and hammered at Jud's midsection. Jud hit him once, hard, directly in the face. Chaskey lumbered back, blood welling from his flattened nose. He looked surprised. The blacks circled around them and shouted. Chaskey rushed, and Jud stepped into the charge. The two men pounded each other about the head and shoulders, clumsily, powerfully, using their fists like clubs. Neither one attempted to disengage. They battered each other in silence, the rhythm of their blows slowing as they tired. Their faces were cut. Above the voices of the watching blacks, Jud heard hoofbeats. Chaskey was weakening, but would not quit. Jud relentlessly bludgeoned the overseer to his knees, and then, absorbing a few harmless blows to his stomach, beat him to the ground. The overseer collapsed and groaned.

There was a commotion on the side. Richard Ackerly pulled his foam-mouthed horse to a stop, and slaves dodged out of the way. He looked down at Chaskey, then at Jud. He smiled.

"You have just killed yourself, nigger."

He ordered Jud brought back to the house. Held by two slaves and flanked by two more, Jud waited in front of the patio while Richard disappeared into the house. Richard returned quickly with Samuel.

Samuel peered into Jud's bruised face. He saw nothing there. Nothing. He did not like that. There should be—well, there *could* be—any one of a number of things. But . . . nothing.

Richard shifted from one foot to the other and back again. His hands twitched at his sides.

"Your buck," he said to his father. He snorted. "He attacked

Chaskey for no reason, no reason at all. He would have killed him if I hadn't arrived in time."

Samuel gazed speculatively at his son. Richard's eyes faltered; he looked to the ground.

Samuel's head bobbed. "Mm-hm. Mm-hm. Yes. All right. Give him fifteen lashes. Then wash him down with brine. We'll send him to Sheol for twelve months, then see what we have."

Book 2

❦

JUD WAS CARTED TO Sheol in the back of an open buck-board. Three slaves carried him to a long shanty and dumped him in a corner. They bolted the door from the outside. Jud lay in perfect darkness; there were no windows.

He was wrapped in a cloth blanket. Beneath the blanket, a gummy bran poultice encased his thighs and back. Two days had passed since his whipping. He had been unconscious most of that time, and they hadn't risked moving him until today. Richard had wielded the bullwhip with a frenzy. When they cut Jud down, they turned him over to an old granny, who mixed and applied the poultice, changing it every hour during the first day—the critical day. While the bran sucked the inflammation and the soaring fever from the boy's body, the old woman bathed his face and limbs continually with cool water, and at intervals forced him up from oblivion, pried his teeth apart with an arthritic finger, and made him drink bitter draughts of tea and crushed herbs.

Sheol was one part of the five-plantation complex—of which Olympus was the nucleus—owned by the Ackerly family. Its Great House, modeled after the one at Olympus, but more modest, was occupied by Harold Goodfriend—Ackerly's deputy—and his family. Other than the overseers' wives or concubines there were no women in Sheol. And no children.

The male slaves, who fluctuated in number between forty and fifty, were drawn from the other four plantations, and they had all been sent to Sheol for correction. Some were balky, others surly, or recalcitrant, or clumsy, or had committed some more than minor offense. Sheol's operating procedure was simple and efficacious: the work load was exhausting, the discipline brutal. Each slave was assigned to Sheol for a specified period of time. At the end of their terms, some were so broken in body and spirit as to be useless to Ackerly, and were sold. Others had learned their lesson and were returned to the plantations from which they'd been sent. Some were given extended terms. A few—the truly wild and incorrigible—were simply killed.

Clanking. Metal grating against metal. A low, growling kind of sound. And in his mouth, dust. He was shuddering, gasping. Cold. He hugged himself. So cold.

Jud woke up. He was lying on his stomach, one side of his face pressed against the chilly, rough wooden floor. He opened his eyes. It was dark. No, not all dark. There was a yellow glow at the end of the room. And between the light and Jud were dark shadowy figures. He heard the clanking of chains again, and the subdued, rumbling growl.

"*Water,*" he said hoarsely.

"Water," someone else said. "He awake an' he want water."

Other voices, distant.

"I thought he dead."

"Pass me that water here."

A wooden bucket was scraped along the floor. It material-
ized in front of him. Jud tried to reach for it but found that he
was bound in a blanket. He worked his way loose and pushed
himself to a half-sitting position. As he did, pointed teeth
seemed to tear flesh from his back. Bursts of color exploded
in his eyes. His teeth chattered. The dipper slipped from his
hand, clattering against the floor. He collapsed.

"Hey, you, stop that soun'."

"You give us all the jitteries, nigger. You soun' like a ghost."

For the first time, Jud heard himself moaning. He tried to
stop.

A chain rattled beside him. A hand went under his head
and raised it, and the wet rim of the dipper was pressed to his
lips.

"Here." The voice was gruff, but the touch was not.
"Drink. You doan fret, boy. You goan be up an' kickin' like
a frisky colt afore long. You all right now. You all right. You
wan' more? Then close yo' eyes. You need sleep-healin' now.
Tha's it. Close yo' eyes."

JUD DIDN'T KNOW HOW long he had slept—minutes,
hours. He awoke in pain. A white man was kneeling over
him, touching him. A candle on the floor made the white
man's face pale, spectral; a demon deciding whether or not
this particular soul was worth the effort of claiming. Beyond
him was another white who held a double-barreled shotgun.
This man's eyes roamed back and forth over the slaves, most

of whom were snoring, some of whom were mumbling, half awakened by the visitors.

"Fever's broke," said the man above Jud. "I think we kin pull off this slime an' let his back git some air. Hol' still there, nigger."

He stripped away the poultice, tossing handfuls to the side, where they lay in a sodden mass.

"Mmph. Looka' that, Chet. They like to snaked him in half. Still wet. Dryin' up round the edges, though. Goddamn! Pret' near ruint his kidney."

The man poked in the right, lower section of Jud's back. Nausea doubled Jud into a ball.

When the men had left, Jud looked out through the long air vents near the ceiling at the stars. He didn't think about anything, and he tried not to feel anything.

THEY WERE AWAKENED BEFORE dawn by two sleepy-eyed slaves who brought them a breakfast of hot mush. The pain was not as bad as it had been the previous night. But Jud was weak, and so stiff he could barely move.

Two oil-rag lamps were burning. The room was bare, with not a single piece of rough furniture. Embers were glowing in the stone fireplace. There were eleven slaves in the shanty including himself. Heavy iron bolts were sunk into the floor, and the slaves wore shackles around their ankles. Four feet of chain linked each of the shackles to one of the bolts. Jud, too, was chained.

Shortly after they had finished breakfast, the two white men Jud had seen the night before entered.

Again, the one called Chet carried a shotgun. The other

one, gaunt, carried a bullwhip, a holstered pistol, and a large key ring. As each slave was freed, he rose and silently left the shanty.

Jud and one other slave remained. "You, Homer," the man with the keys said, "you work with Mista Atwood's gang to-day."

"Yes, suh, Masta Collins."

It was the same rough voice Jud had heard when he'd been helped to drink.

Homer left. Collins turned the key in Jud's shackle. He glanced without real interest at Jud's back, grunting to himself.

"Pick up them dirty pans an' come with me."

Jud gathered the pans slowly, wincing as he moved, and stifling little gasps. Collins brandished the whip.

"Be spry! If'n you don' work that soreness out, you stiffen up an' be crippled sure. Bend over all the way!"

At the door, Jud paused to let Collins precede him. The overseer pushed him forward.

"Go on. Ain't no nigger that gets behind a white man here for *no* reason."

Outside it was hazy and the sky was dirty gray with the first light of false dawn. The night chill was still in the air. Slaves were stamping their feet, hugging themselves, and rubbing their sides. They stood in groups of ten. Each group was shepherded by a white man. All the overseers were armed. A few slaves were passing out canvas seed bags with shoulder straps.

"Caesar," Collins called.

A chestnut-colored slave jerked his head up.

"Yassum. Yes, suh, Mista Collins, Masta."

His seed bag fell to the ground, spilling most of its contents. Caesar plunged to his hands and knees, scrambled in the dirt, and scooped up the seeds with rapid, jerky motions.

"I's sorry, Masta Wilkey," he wailed to the nearest overseer. "I din' mean no harm. I cleans 'em up good. I git ever' one of 'em. See? See? I comin', Masta Collins."

He howled when Wilkey kicked him.

"Oh, don' snake Caesar's black ass. I scamper like a squirrel all day. I work extry hard."

He spun and crawled like a running, handicapped dog to Collins. He gained his feet halfway and loped the rest of the distance.

"I here, Masta. I here jus' as lightnin' fas' as my pore black body kin move. Whut you wants Caesar to do, suh? You jus' tell 'im an' it be done."

Jud's eyes would not stay on Caesar's face. He looked up to the sky. Some stars were still visible. Faint, but hard, points of light. The moon was pale. He studied it.

A voice to the side muttered something. The only word Jud caught was "Caesar." Then there was the sound of someone spitting.

"You jest lookin' for a lead ball in your head, ain't you, nigger?" said Wilkey.

Jud looked and saw that the overseer had uncoiled his whip. He was squinting at a huge slave—the largest man Jud had ever seen. The black stepped away from the rest of the slaves and faced Wilkey. He was several inches taller than Jud, and massive. His head was outsized even for his body, and deformed, roughly the girth and shape of a young watermelon.

His eyes were bulbous, froglike. A vivid red scar ran from his forehead to his chin, cutting his face into two unequal halves.

"You know whut I a-goin' to do to you someday?" Wilkey said, tone conversational, almost amiable. "When your term up, I goin' to give a full report to Mista Ackerly an' he goin' to say, 'Wilkey, my fren', you take that nigger out behind the barn an' you shoot him dead.' An' that jus' whut I goin' to do. I goin' to blow a hole clean through you an' they ain't goin' to be nothin' but mush-meat where your heart used to be. That's whut we do to mad dogs, an' that's whut we do to mad niggers."

The whip flicked back, then sliced the air and tore a patch from Shadrach's shirt, laying a crimson welt on his side. Shadrach didn't move. Wilkey swung the whip around his head with casual expertise, and struck again. As Shadrach waited for the next blow, he was struck from behind by the whip of another overseer. He spun, was lashed by Wilkey. The whites laid into Shadrach from both sides with a rhythm. Shadrach's arms rose, and for a moment it looked as if he would seize both whips and yank them away. Then he clenched his fists, his biceps swelled, then swelled again, and his chest expanded, and his face was transfigured into a thing that was at once both wrathful and rapturous.

"All right," said Collins. "That's enuff. Don' cut him so he can't work."

Shadrach was bleeding in several spots. Puffy ridges were rising on his skin.

"Whut you standin' there for?" Wilkey said.

Shadrach smiled. "You din' tell me to do nothin' else, Masta."

"Git on back with them other niggers."

"Yes, suh, Masta. Yes, suh."

Shadrach moved slowly, ponderously, back into the ranks. Wilkey ordered his crew out to the fields. The other groups followed at intervals. Collins said to Caesar, "You watch over this buck today, hear? You show him what to do. Keep him movin'—a lot o' bendin' an' a lot o' liftin'. Don' want him cripplin' up on us. If he ain't limber by the end of the day, you the one that goin' get the hidin'. You unnerstan'?"

"Yes, suh, Masta. I git him limbry like a snake. You jus' de-pen' on ol' Caesar."

"I am."

Collins pointed the butt of his whip at Caesar. The black winced.

First they gathered all the tin plates from the shanties. They filled two barrels with hot water, scrubbed the plates with pumice stones, and set them on the ground to dry in the sun. Next they washed and dried the crockery and uten-sils from the overseers' homes and the china from the Great House. There were iron ovens from which the ashes had to be removed. There was firewood to carry and stack.

The hard scabs on Jud's back tore loose around the edg-es and a clear liquid oozed out. But by late afternoon he was feeling better for his activity, looser. Caesar implored, cajoled, begged him to work harder and faster, and whenever an over-seer passed the smaller man cowered.

Jud kept as far from him as was possible. He thought about this. He had never, so far as he knew, either liked or disliked anybody. Maybe disliking somebody meant that you didn't want to be near them. Maybe he disliked Caesar.

Something was wrong inside him. He stared into the sky awhile; he focused on a stark-white, ragged cloud, tried to float with it through the blue emptiness, tried to be nothing.

He couldn't. Not completely.

His stomach tightened periodically, and sometimes sweat broke out on his palms.

Maybe he was afraid.

Of what?

Darkness had nearly swallowed Sheol before the slaves were returned to their shanties and chained for the night. Collins left a bottle of fish oil with Jud, telling him to rub it into the scabs; this would keep them pliable so the wounds would not tear and reopen each day. Most of Jud's back had not scabbed over. Instead it had ridged and hardened, as the flesh does when a fingertip has been injured and the dead nail falls away. This process was incomplete, and there were still wet and raw patches. Jud contorted himself to apply the oil, but there were areas he could not reach.

"Gimme that skunk juice," said Homer.

Jud handed him the bottle. Homer's blunt fingers rubbed the oil on sparingly and quickly. His touch was like his voice, rough but not hard. He capped the bottle.

"There. Now maybe you won't wriggle around so much, an' I kin git some rest."

Jud said nothing. Supper had been finished and there was a heavy somnolence in the air. The slaves were not sleeping, though.

Homer sighed. He was not old, but his face was grizzled. His features were ill-defined, seeming to flow into each other.

There were thin lines etched into the skin about his mouth and eyes, as if he were in perpetual pain.

A slave began to sing to himself, low-voiced, melodic. A subdued conversation started at the far end of the shanty. Chains rattled.

"I gettin' out of here soon," someone said. "Masta Goodfriend tell me today. Ain't goan have no chain on my leg no more."

"How soon?"

"My fingers on bof han's an' my toes on one foot."

"*Mm-hm.* That nice. That real nice."

A flat voice said: "Ain't no nigger never get out of no-place. 'Cep' by dyin'. A grave be the only thing that love a nigger. Fold him up nice an' snug, keep him warm in the winter an' cool in the summer."

"Grave ain't goan love you no more'n a white man do. It goan eat you up, fill your mouf wif worms," Shadrach said. "Not even niggers love niggers."

Then there was silence, broken only by the slave who was singing to himself. Jud listened. He *wanted* the others to speak. When he realized this, his stomach began to twitch. What was wrong? What was happening to him? He lay back and tried to listen to the sound within his head. He couldn't.

The slave who had been singing stopped. "I'm goan run," he said.

"Whut?"

"You cain't run from here."

"I ain't goan run from here. If'n I behave, they goan take me 'way from here 'bout the time the firs' bloom come on the plants, near as I kin reckon. When I gets back, I show Mista

Ackerly that I a *re*-formed nigger. I used drive a team fo' him, pick up things from Europa an' his other plantations, bring 'em back to Olympus. Take me a entire day, it used to.

"Well, suh, I goan set out one mornin' an I jus' goan keep on till night come. Then I goan hide the buckboard an' I goan keep to the woods, walk by the moon, an' sleep during the day."

"Where you goan go?"

"North."

"Whut you goan do when you gits there?"

"Work fo' wages."

Homer said, "They catch you 'fore you get fifty mile. Ain't *no* way fo' a nigger to get North from down here. No way at all."

"But if you go South," someone said, "an' if you kin git as fur as Charleston, you might git free."

Homer laughed brittlely. "Nobody in Charleston goan free no nigger. More likely they hang you up by your heels."

"No, they people there that help niggers. They called Quakers. The men wear long dark coats an' the ladies got dresses so long that even their shoes is covered. When they talk, it sound like a preacher-man readin' out of a Bible. They got meetin' houses where they go sit an' talk all night about freein' niggers."

"An' they white?"

"They white as Masta's linen."

"That crazy. I never heard nuffin' so crazy!"

"It true. I tell you it true. My ol' masta brung me to Charleston wif his fambly once. An' I saw 'em wif my own two eyes. Masta push one off the boardwalk right into the mud an' cuss him out fit to pop a blood vessy. But the gen-nelman in the long coat, he doan say nuffin'. He jus' smile at Masta all kind-like. He tip his hat at Masta's wife an' say, 'Good day,' an' he walk away."

"He scared of your masta, tha's all."

"No, he weren't. He a big man, an' my ol' masta only a little mitey thing."

"How these Quakers make you free?" Homer challenged.

"They hides you somehow an' they gits you up North."

"North!" Shadrach rumbled. "They got white men up North?"

"Why sure they got white men. Whut the matter wif you, Shadrach? Doan you know nuffin'?"

"I know more'n you, nigger. I know they got laws up North that make 'em bring niggers back to the mastas they run from. An' I know they got white men there who doan do nuffin' else but hunt down runners an' bring 'em back South for *re*-wards. I know I run from Virginy when I hardly more'n a saplin'. I know I live in New York two weeks an' nobody give me no work an' I starve half-dead. An' I know they arres' me an' beat me so my ear doan work an' my eyes go flippy an' they bring me back to Virginy."

"It different. It not all the same."

"White men are white men," Shadrach said.

"Sometimes these Quakers git you up to Cany-da."

"What that?" Jud asked without realizing he was doing so. He was surprised by the sound of his voice.

"Cany-da a place that . . . well . . . it not the South, but it not the North. It a different place. They doan got slaves there. Nary a one."

"You dreamin'," someone said. "Ain't no place where they ain't some kind of slave."

"Tha's right," Homer said savagely. "They's slaves ev-er'where you go. They ain't nothin' you kin do. *Nothin'!*" He slumped back against the wall.

"I gots to be free!" said the black who claimed he was go-ing to run.

Homer spoke to himself. Only Jud heard him.

"It hard. Oh, Lordy, it pow'ful hard." He made a choked sound in his throat.

"I *gots* to be free!"

Free. Jud's mouth was dry, his throat constricted. Breathing was difficult. What was happening to him? *What?*

He knuckled his hand into a fist and struck the floor.

The sound boomed in the shanty, silencing the blacks.

In a moment, Shadrach said: "Tha's free. Tha's how you git free. The *only* way. Free doan mean nothin' but one thing—not havin' no masta. Tha's all. Nothin' more. An' as long as they's white men, you not goan be free. You wan' be free . . . then kill the white man! Kill ever' one! Kill 'em!"

"Shut your mouf, Shadrach." An urgent voice. "They goan hear you an' come in here an' rip us all to pieces."

"Kill the white man!" Shadrach roared.

"Wif whips," someone said. "Snake 'em all to death."

"Snake 'em," Shadrach said. "Shoot 'em, bash they heads an' pull they brains out, cut 'em, burn 'em—it doan make no difference, but kill 'em. Kill 'em!"

"Tear they *throats* out," chanted a wiry mulatto.

"*Kill 'em!*" answered Shadrach.

"Gouge they *eyes* out."

"*Kill 'em!*"

"Smash they *heads* in."

"*Kill 'em!*" Shadrach's voice was not alone.

"Cut they *balls* off."

"*Kill 'em!*"

"Carve they *hearts* up."

"*Kill 'em!*"

"Kill them!" shouted the mulatto.

The moment was poised, full, fiery. A word, a scream, and half of the shanty's blacks would have set to clawing and jerking at their chains, would have torn their fingernails and ripped their flesh against the cold iron. The others were cowering in the darkness. Jud belonged to neither side. He was disembodied, spiraling, leaping—a leaf driven by a howling autumn wind. He shook.

Silence. Long, long empty silence. And then a plunge into darkness.

The chains were strong. And too many. Oh, so many! How did you carry me in your dark wet cave, Mammy, when I was so heavy with chains?

Silence.

Shadrach buried his face in his hands with a moan. He doubled over, rocked back and forth, and wept.

TWO WEEKS AFTER THE last of the seed had been put into the ground, the first tender, pale green shoots forced their way up from the dirt and struggled toward the sky. The dark fields wore these like a shy girl donning finery for the first time. As soon as the shoots had unfurled their third leaves, the slaves trooped out to the fields with hoes and spades and dirt forks. Painstakingly, they set to clearing the ridges of the weeds that had sprung up beside the cotton. This care was required daily during the first month. As the plants grew hardier, bulltongues—narrow plows—were used to turn loose earth around the ridges and bury grass and small corn plants that had continued to grow. Since dray animals could no longer be used for fear of trampling the cotton, slaves were harnessed to the bulltongues.

The sun burned, sweat glistened, and muscles strained. There were irrigation canals to be dug when the ground grew dry. There were aphids to destroy, and leaf worms, bollworms, thrips and spider mites. The cotton plants were coaxed, nourished, prayed to. And bled for.

Jud's back healed into corrugated, horny scar tissue. There remained an ache in his kidney. This grew progressively less noticeable, as his body accustomed itself to it. Occasionally it would blossom, making him limp slightly.

He worked hard, pushing himself. By the end of the day, he was barely able to stagger back to the shanty. But it did little good. It did not kill the thing inside him that made him hungry to hear the others speak, that made him clench and unclench his fists while his mouth worked wordlessly, that prevented him from listening to the sound within his head.

New blacks arrived at Sheol, some unmarked, some mutilated, some bloodied by the snake. One was brought in a buckboard, unconscious, his back even more torn than Jud's had been. He died during the night, and Jud and another slave dragged his body to the large burial area—devoid of stones or markers—at the edge of the woods. They began to dig, uncovered the leg of a corpse in advanced putrefaction, shifted the site, and buried the new carcass in a shallow grave after pushing to the side the yellowish bones they found there.

A few slaves were returned to the plantations from which they had been sent. They whooped and laughed as they left.

With the ceaseless attention given to the cotton, Sheol's grounds and buildings had fallen into disrepair and neglect. Goodfriend judged that the plants could safely be left untended for a day, and the slaves were put to work on the plantation proper. Jud was working on the chimney at one of the overseers' homes. With him were Caesar and another slave. Caesar's term had expired more than a week ago. He had not been told yet what was going to be done with him. He was whining and petulant, and broke into tears often. He was terrified of Wilkey. Several times the white man had approached Caesar, stroked his shotgun, and said gravely, "Well, nigger, Mista Ackerly finally tol' me whut to do with you. Come on, you an' me are goin' to take a little walk out behind the barn."

Caesar would fall to his knees screaming.

Wilkey would walk away guffawing.

At midday, Goodfriend appeared. With him were an older man in a broadcloth coat and a pudgy little boy with red cheeks. The boy kept tugging at his father's hand, trying to gain his attention. The party came to a halt.

The boy jumped up and down, clapping his hands. A few blacks—not many—grinned and waved at him.

"Which one?" he squealed. "Which one, huh, Daddy? Which one?"

His father looked questioningly to Goodfriend. Goodfriend pointed.

"Hey, you Caesar. Get on down here."

Caesar scrambled across the roof of the overseer's house and clambered down the ladder.

"Yes, suh. Yes, Masta, I's here." His head bobbed up and down. He wrung his hands.

"That's him," Goodfriend said.

"Kin he do tricks like Scroomey?"

"Scroomey?" Goodfriend asked.

"The boy's dog," answered the man. "Died a while back. Calvin got the notion into his haid that he wanted a nigger this time 'stead of another dog. Ain't none of our own bucks really fit for what the boy has in mind."

Goodfriend nodded. "Sure he can do tricks. Caesar, you do just what that boy tells you, hear?"

"Yassum. Yes, suh, Masta."

Calvin danced from foot to foot. Caesar waited.

"Sit!" the boy cried suddenly.

Caesar sat.

"Roll over."

Caesar complied. The boy giggled.

"Now . . . play dead!"

Caesar lay motionless.

"No-no-no!" Calvin screamed. "With big white eyes an' your tongue floppin' out an' your arms an' legs sticked up in the air."

When Caesar mastered the position, Calvin pointed and called, "Dead nigger, dead nigger. See, Daddy?"

Jud, atop the roof, looked away. He looked out across the fields, to the trees, to the horizon. It wasn't enough. He looked up to the sky. Then he forced his vision directly into the blinding white heart of the sun. His eyes watered immediately; his lids struggled to close themselves. He was unable to stop the instinctive bunching of his muscles which wrenched his head to the side. For a few moments he could see nothing but whiteness.

Caesar was still playing dead. Calvin stood beside him, gnawing on his upper lip.

"I cain't think of what to have him *do,*" the boy wailed.

"Well," said his father, "what do you want him to do?"

"I don' *know!*"

"Fetch a stick, maybe?"

"No. What good's a nigger if he cain't do no more'n Scroomey could?"

"Get him to ride you around," the boy's father suggested.

Calvin picked up a piece of lath from the ground and had Caesar crouch so he could climb up on the black's shoulders. The ride exhilarated the boy. He threw back his head and laughed, struck the black with the piece of lath, and yelled, "Faster. Faster."

Caesar broke into a shambling run, a parody of a gallop. They finished the ride. Calvin dismounted and ran to his father.

"I want him, Daddy. Kin I have him? Please, Daddy?"

"You're sure now?"

Calvin nodded. "He ain't awful bright, but he moves fast. I can learn him lots of tricks."

"How much you want for him?" the man asked Goodfriend.

"Three hundred fifty."

"That's a mite steep for a toy."

Goodfriend stroked his jaw. "Aren't going to find a buck

that your boy can handle as easy as this one, and, if you really need him, he's not completely ruint as a worker."

"Daddy, he kin eat an' drink out'n Scroomey's old dishes, cain't he? An' it's all right if I give him the leavin's from my plate, ain't it?"

At the mention of leavings, Caesar's face seemed to illuminate itself. He dropped to his knees in front of Calvin.

"I be a good nigger fo' you, Masta. Caesar be the right fittest nigger you ever see. I put your ol' houn' dog to shame. I be twice as perky an' I learn mo' tricks than all the smartes' houn's in the world."

Calvin rubbed the black's hair. "We kin put Scroomey's old collar roun' his neck too, huh, Daddy?"

"Well," the man said to Goodfriend, "how 'bout three hundred even?"

"Since the boy's heart's set, I suppose I could come down to three twenty-five."

Calvin found a length of rope amid a pile of harnesses that had been brought out to be oiled. He tied one end around Caesar's neck and clutched the other end in his small fist.

The man laughed and tousled his son's hair. "All right. Three twenty-five it is."

"We'll go back to the house, and I'll draw up a bill of sale for you."

They left. Calvin followed them, tugging Caesar along after him.

"Bark," Calvin said.

Caesar grinned. "Arf. Arf-arf."

THE MORNINGS CAME, YANKED the slaves from their dreams, and matured into bright searing days that rolled over them like millstones and then faded and left them to sink into stuporous sleep again. The cotton plants thrived. Straps welted skin. New faces appeared; old ones left. There was not much sense of either gain or loss.

The ground was not the same. The sky was not the same. Everything was strange. The earth was hard beneath Jud's feet; it would not let him sink into it. The sky weighted down upon him; it would not let him rise to float insensate through the vaporous clouds. He felt the impact of the hoe striking the dirt. The cotton plants scraped his skin. The boards on which he slept were hard. At every moment, at every place, something assaulted him.

The sound in his head had died; he could not hear it, no matter how intently he listened.

At night in the shanty, he narrowed his eyes, trying to pierce the gloom that encompassed all but the areas around the two small oil lamps, trying to see the faces of the blacks who spoke. It was dark in his corner. No one saw the way his mouth opened, sometimes forming silent words. No one saw him sitting erect—after most of the others had gone to sleep—listening, hoping.

"It a lot," he said one night.

Homer turned. "You say somethin', boy?"

"It a lot."

"What?"

"I don' know. Ever'thin' . . . nothin'. It—I don' know."

"Make sense, nigger. You all sudden learn how to talk,

it ain't goan do you much good if'n you doan make sense. Whut you sayin'?"

"I don' know what it all about."

"You doan know whut *whut* all about?"

"Ever'thin."

"The sun fry your brains in the field, boy?"

Jud was silent.

"Ever'thin," Homer muttered. "Nothin'. Your brains boiled sure. I cain't unnerstan' you nohow. Hey, doan look at me like that. Whut the matter wif you, boy?" Homer peered into Jud's face; then he shook his head. "All right. All right. Ever'thin's about nothin'. Nothin'. Tha's whut ever'thin' is. Nothin' doan ever change. The sun come up, the nigger work the field, an' the white man hol' the whip. But it ain't nothin', you unnerstan'?" His voice grew angry. "Nothin' ain't nothin'! Now leave me alone, you crazy nigger."

Homer turned his back. Jud sat with his hands folded in his lap, his shoulders slumped. After a moment, he reached out and touched Homer on the shoulder.

"I tol' you to leave me alone."

"I want to . . . to talk."

"Cain't make no sense outta your talk." He looked at Jud. "Nobody doan wan' lissen to no nigger that . . . Oh, all right! Go on, talk. But make sense."

"I . . . I . . ." Jud lifted his hands helplessly.

Homer put a forearm across his eyes, rubbed, then said quietly, "It all right, boy. Now you jus' think a minute, then you tell Homer about your mammy—if you ever knowed her—an' about where you growed up. You jus' think a minute, then you talk. Homer lissen to you. Much as you wan'."

THE BLOOM BEGAN IN the morning, a few hours after dawn. The buds opened into wet and crinkled petals that spread under the heat of the sun, grew full, and emitted a heavy fragrance. By noon the fields were carpeted with the white flowers. As the afternoon wore on, faint reddish streaks appeared in the petals, lengthened, and grew darker. When the slaves arrived the next morning the thousands upon thousands of flowers were a pure, clear pink.

Surrounded by the blossoms, Jud felt good as he worked. Jud had never sung in his life, but today he hummed. The flowers began to wither about noon. They died, and the dry petals dropped to the earth, to be ground underfoot. Brief, beautiful, brilliant lives. Jud's eyes teared. He grew careless, damaging several of the denuded cotton plants.

ALEX, THE SLAVE WHO'D said he was going to steal a buckboard from Olympus and run, was brought back to Sheol less than a week after he'd been returned to Olympus. He'd been beaten by the bounty hunters who had captured him on his second day of freedom and carted him, chained and unconscious, back to Ackerly for the reward. He was bruised, lacerated, and unable to use his right arm. He refused to eat. Collins and Wilkey fed him by force, but later he regurgitated everything he had swallowed. The slaves woke one morning to find him stiff and unmoving. Homer was one of the slaves assigned to the burial. Alex's spindly and shrunken body was not dragged to the grave. Homer carried it, cradled in his arms.

Shadrach had not spoken much since the day Caesar had been sold. The elephantine black sweated, ate, and rested in silence. Wilkey baited him, but Shadrach gave the overseer no satisfaction.

The cotton bolls formed with their tough leathery skin. The sun grew ferocious, and the blacks worked stripped to their waists. A slave from Wilkey's group had gulped too much water at midday meal and had fallen into a seizure and been carried back to the shanties. Collins's group was working nearby, and Shadrach had been transferred to Wilkey. It was hot, quiet work—no sounds save the occasional snap of a strap, a moan, grunts, and the white men telling the slaves to move on to the next row, to work harder, to work faster . . . .

"Kill the white man!"

Jud stopped in midstroke and looked up. The figures around him were frozen. It was not real: *Kill the white man?*

The bellow rolled over the field a second time: "Kill the white man!"

Shadrach was standing spread-legged in front of Wilkey, holding his hoe high, like a staff. The overseer wore an expression of bewilderment.

The hoe seemed to Jud to remain suspended for a very long time.

"Wilkey!" Collins shouted.

Wilkey swung his shotgun as the hoe began its rapid arc down. The hoe ripped Wilkey's shoulder and struck the gun. The weapon discharged, but its load smashed into the ground and the gun was knocked from Wilkey's hands.

Collins drew his pistol and aimed at Shadrach.

"Kill the white man!" shouted a man behind Jud.

Collins spun and covered his blacks. "The firs' nigger t' move is a dead nigger."

Wilkey's own pistol was in his hand.

"Kill him!" shouted one of Wilkey's slaves.

Another hoe slashed down. Wilkey screamed. The pistol was gone. His hand dangled from his wrist. Bright red blood spouted over the cotton plants. Shadrach struck again and a crimson line streaked across the overseer's face. Then there were four slaves chopping at the white man, screaming.

In the distance there were other shouts, and dull reports of firearms.

Wilkey stumbled back, was rushed and hacked. He fell and disappeared between two rows of plants. The hoes rose and plunged. Blood sprayed into the air. Shadrach flung aside his stained hoe.

"Kill 'em!" he shouted. "Run!"

He crashed through the cotton rows toward the woods. A handful of others followed. The rest dropped their tools and stood trembling, mouths gaping.

"Kill the white man!" Homer cried hoarsely at Jud's side.

He rushed forward, swinging his hoe. Two slaves went with him. Collins stepped quickly back.

"Hold it! Hold it!" he shouted.

Homer aimed a blow at Collins's throat. Collins fired. Homer's head blew apart and he spun and fell into the cotton plants. Collins went down beneath the hoes of the other two slaves. Then they ran toward the woods.

Jud looked across the field. There were several blacks churning through the cotton toward freedom. Most of the groups were still intact, though, their overseers holding them at bay with leveled weapons. There were a few clusters of slaves standing alone.

In front of Jud, hidden by the cotton plants, Collins groaned. Jud stepped forward, tightening his grip around his hoe. The white man was lying on his back. His head, and chest were cut and bleeding profusely. His eyes were wide and fearful. His torn lips twitched. His head jerked. Jud stood above him and looked down.

Kill the white man.

He could, he realized suddenly. It was not simply an opportunity; he was *capable* of doing it.

He raised the hoe. Collins whimpered.

Freedom. His arms shook. And death soon after. Shadrach and the others were dead. The whites could not permit them to live.

Why had Homer charged, knowing he had no chance, that Collins would kill him?

Did Jud want to live? He didn't know.

And he didn't know if he wanted to die.

Beneath Jud's hoe, Collins was whimpering. The white man fouled his clothes. Jud dropped the hoe, bent, and reached. The overseer closed his eyes and screamed. Jud worked his hands under Collins's shoulders and legs, and lifted him.

He was not conscious of the weight of his burden, only of the white man sobbing against his broad, dark chest.

"It goin' be all right," he said tonelessly.

He walked toward the Great House.

Book 3

❦

SAMUEL WAS SITTING ON the veranda smoking and reading a paper when Jud was brought to Olympus's Great House. Samuel looked up with puzzlement.

The creases in the white man's face had deepened since Jud had last seen him. His hair had grown thinner. His blue eyes seemed paler and the compact fortress that was his body seemed to have been battered. Ackerly stroked his jaw and peered from Jud to the overseer who had brought him, Sloan.

"Yes?"

Sloan cleared his throat. "Uh, this here's Jud, Mista Ackerly. I brung him to you like Mista Goodfriend said I should."

"Jud. Jud. Ah. Yes. Well, boy. How have you been doing these last months?"

Jud shifted his shoulders and nodded.

"Uhm. Yes, good. Did they work that devilment out of you? No more brawling?" Then, without waiting, he continued, "About Collins. Good, very good. Shows character. Knew you had the makings of a good nigger in you. Just a matter of bringing it out. All right, Sloan. Take him down to the smith's and get those chains removed. Tell Goodfriend I have commuted his punishment and that he'll be staying here."

Sloan touched his hat brim. "Yes, suh."

"Oh, Sloan."

"Suh?"

"Tell Goodfriend I just learned that they caught three more of those black butchers near Foreston. Snaked them to death in front of the town hall. No word on that big one yet."

"Yes, suh."

They left. Samuel returned to his paper.

It was that madman Lincoln, and talk of secession. He set down the paper and sighed. He was tired. He always seemed tired these days.

"Samuel? Samuel!" shrilled Amanda from within the house. "Where are you? I want to talk to you."

He rose with a grunt and stood facing the door a moment; then he backed to the stairs, went down from the veranda, and shambled across the lawn to the side of the house, moving out toward the shanties.

WHEN THE BOLTS WERE struck off and the shackles removed, Jud rubbed his wrists, and clenched and unclenched his hands. He walked out of the smithy and stood blinking in the sunlight. No one paid any attention to him. He felt vaguely uneasy; he hunched his shoulders without realizing it, anticipating a shout and a quick blow.

"Jud. Hey, Jud. It you. I knowed it you. Ain't nobody else here so black."

It was Plum, grinning broadly, the only marked nigger

Richard had bought the day of the Memphis auction. He clapped a hand to Jud's shoulder.

"Um-um." His fingers felt the welts under Jud's shirt. "The way they mark you, it seem like I ain't hardly ever been touched. But I bets they whupped that ol' demon outta you. Yes, suh, they surely must, else'n you wouldn't be here now. Praise the Lord that demon been *ex-or-cised*. The Lord watch ovuh his chillen, he certainly do."

"How you gettin' on, Plum?"

"Pow'ful good. Jesus bin walkin' by my side evuh since he strike my ol' masta down an' cause Mista Richard to buy me an' my brother up. That the day of our deliverance, it surely were. We put our trust in the Lord, an' he walk wif us—be our shield an' our staff—fo' the rest of our natural-born days."

He stood back and eyed Jud critically. "You come to Jesus? You bin baptized?"

Jud shook his head.

"Well, we gots to rectify that. Yes, suh, we surely do. I kin baptize, you know. I a deacon now in the Lord's service. They's this preacher in Turbeville who travels all aroun' these parts, stayin' two, three days wif the plantation owners and preachin' to they niggers. Well, jus' after the firs' shoots come up in the fields, he write to all the white folks an' say he goan run a small school a li'l while, teach one nigger from each plantation how to preach the word, how to baptize, an' how to feed the niggers' hungry souls. He got rich white ladies in his flock that offer to pay the mastas fo' the time the niggers be away from the fields. Masta Samuel sen' me, an' I learn stories from the Bible, an' I learn how to baptize an' all the right words—"

Plum's gaze drifted up to the sky. "An' I learn about heaven, an' all about the sweet, the oh so sweet love of Jesus.

"An' me an' Harris, we fall on our knees an' we thanks the Lord ever' mornin' an' night fo' our deliverance, an' fo' keepin' our bodies an' souls safe from harm." His eyes swept back to Jud. "But you gots to earn the Lord's love. You gots to rid you'se'f of Satan an' his legions of demons. 'Cause Jesus doan love no contrary nigger, He doan love an' He doan protec' no troublesome buck. So you clean yo' house, like the Bible say, an' then I takes you down to the rivuh an' bring God to you jus' like John the Baptist, an' then Jesus be yo' shield an' staff, too."

Plum took Jud by both shoulders. "You hear?"

Jud nodded.

"Then you make yo'se'f ready." He paused. "It good to have you back, brother, now that the craziness gone outta you."

Jud went to the carpentry shop. He was glad Plum had recognized him, had called him by name and stopped to talk.

Fires were burning beneath iron kettles set atop brick supports. In these kettles clothes were being boiled in soapy water. Four female slaves worked the clothes with long wooden poles, steam and sweat plastering their wet frocks to their bodies. Jud glanced at them, opened the door to the shop, and paused and looked back. One of them had black and tightly waved hair that glistened in the sun.

He remembered her. She was Delia, the girl who had been purchased shortly before his fight with Chaskey, the one who had sat in front of him the time Reverend Hartwell had preached to them.

Her body was fuller now, but still unfinished. She was not

tall, but she held her head high on her slim neck. She gave the impression that at this moment—in any other place imaginable—she would be doing exactly the same thing, simply because she *wished* to do so.

Jud watched her body strain to meet a work load beyond her strength, watched her metal-hard determination.

He went inside the shop. It was empty. There was an unfinished wheel-hub on the workbench. Jud turned it over in his hands. The original block had not been cut properly; it was unbalanced. However, it could be salvaged. He took up a reaming instrument and set to work. As he cut away at the hard wood, he thought about the girl Delia.

SAMUEL WALKED THROUGH THE slave quarters and work buildings with his hands jammed in his pockets. In the smokehouse, he rapped a sleeping slave sharply on the head with his knuckles. The black awoke with a startled cry.

"Please, Masta Samuel, suh," he begged. "Doan whup Lenny, suh. I jus' close my eyes the briefes' li'l secon' to res' my pore achin' head. I got a pow'ful pain there, suh. I not sleepin', suh. I surely not."

"Yes. Yes. You don't even sleep at night. I know. Well, the afternoon is getting on. You'd better carry those hams over to the larder."

"Yassum. Yes, suh! Lenny skitter these ham ovuh faster'n hot grease."

Samuel rapped the black on the head again, sportively.

In the stables, Samuel spoke to no one. He stood off to the side, muttered to himself, and thought about taking a horse and riding out to look at the cotton gangs.

He shook his head: "No. Too hot. Too hot."

He wandered about without any particular goal or direction.

"'Noon, Mista Samuel," a black called. "Did Mista Richard cotch that Shadrach yet?"

"Not yet. Soon, soon, I imagine."

"Oooh-*ee!* They goan skin that ol' nigguh alive."

"Yes. They will."

Samuel had placed a bounty on each of the rebellious blacks. Militia-like units were sweeping through South Carolina and the border areas of the neighboring states. From the larger plantations, every white adult male who could be spared had armed himself and saddled a horse. A general uprising of slaves—though unlikely—would be disastrous, and the seeds had to be crushed. No gentleman, of course, would ever claim the bounty on such a nigger. But the reward did draw hordes of vagrants and poor whites into the affair—anyone who could lay hands on a firearm, or fashion a nail-studded club. Three days had passed, and already sixteen of the twenty-one fugitives had been killed—and an unfortunate, regrettable number of innocent niggers too.

Richard had participated in three of the kills, but as yet his primary and declared quarry, Shadrach, was still at large.

Samuel wished that Richard would come home. It was difficult to maintain even an armed truce with Amanda while the boy was away. Since Maybelle had come to Olympus, well . . .

Samuel kicked at a stone and sighed. Tired, he was just too damn tired.

He came upon the boiling clothes.

"Emerald!"

A fat middle-aged slave snapped her head up.

"Yes, Masta?"

"Why have you got the girl working here?" He pointed to Delia. "This work is too heavy for her."

"She ain't no striplin' no more, Masta. She pret' near growed. But if'n you say so . . ."

Delia continued to stir the clothes in the kettle with a slow rhythm.

"Girl," said Samuel, his voice gruff, "is this wearing you down any?"

"No, suh. It not too hard."

Samuel coughed. "All right, then."

He walked to the nearest shanty, sat down on a three-legged stool, tipped it back so that it stood on two legs, and leaned against the wall. He packed his pipe with tobacco, lit it, and pulled silently. He watched Delia work.

A beautiful little creature. A nigger, a black nigger wench, but still she was—beautiful. Like a moth. Like a thin-stemmed crystal goblet.

Like a daughter . . .

He got up abruptly, kicked away the stool, and left. Tired. Christ, so tired.

JUD EMERGED FROM THE carpentry shop at suppertime. Blacks were sauntering leisurely toward their shanties. They stretched as they walked, poked each other in fun, made jokes, and laughed with great hee-hawing sounds. Amid the dark skins, the gray, tattered work clothes, and the drab buildings, moved a burst of color—a young woman in a pale blue dress with a tight bodice and a flaring bell-shaped skirt. Her hair was elaborately coifed and held with jeweled combs. It was black hair with wide, premature swaths of white in it. Her decolletage was low, and her shoulders bare. She was laughing. Now and then she reached down and swatted the naked buttocks of a passing child with her closed fan. Then her wrist would flick and the fan would spring open and flutter over her mouth and nose as her eyes darted around. The slaves laughed nervously: "That Miss Maybelle, she sure . . . she sure . . . Um!"

Plum fell into step beside Jud. He looked sorrowfully at the woman.

"Who is she?" Jud said.

"Mist'ess 'Manda's kin. She a widow-woman. Her husband, he—" Plum lowered his voice. "They say he shoot his own head off. Um! Miss Maybelle come here roun' seedin' time all dressed in black. She bin here ever since."

Maybelle swung in their direction. Plum stopped short. Maybelle closed the distance quickly, skirt caught up in her hand, a few inches of white stocking showing above her ankles.

"Now, Plum," she said, "why do you look at me like that? Do I give you a fright, honey?" She poked him in the ribs with her fan. "Land's sake. An itty thing like me giving the scaries to a big boy like you? Why, Plum, it just isn't natural, I tell you. You afraid I'll eat you up?"

Plum pawed at the ground with one bare foot. He swallowed, and his larynx bobbed.

"My, my. Why, who on earth is your friend, Plum? He's

a big one, isn't he? Makes you look almost puny, which of course you're far from being. What's your name?"

"Jud, ma'am."

"Jud. That's nice, real nice. It fits you. Nothing wasted, strong. Well, Jud, are you afraid of me too?"

"No, ma'am."

Maybelle smiled. "That's wonderful!" She peeped at him from behind her fan. "All the others are. Tell me, Jud, why *aren't* you afraid of me?"

"I don' know, ma'am."

"Oh, that's precious! What are you afraid of, Jud?"

"I don't know, ma'am."

"Do you mean you're afraid of something you don't understand, or that there's nothing at all that frightens you?"

"I can't think of nothin', ma'am."

"How absolutely marvelous. A nigger who isn't afraid of anything. You are a very, very rare thing, Jud. Well, I imagine that if I were as big as you are and as strong as you look, I would be a little less fearful myself." She laughed. "You two dears run along now and get yourselves some supper. Big men need to eat regularly. 'Bye, now."

She spun away with a swishing of her skirt.

Chaskey had sought Jud out earlier in the day. The foreman's nose was flat and crooked, there was a half-moon scar under his right eye, and one of his ears was larger than the other.

"Hey, Jud, you coal-nigger."

Jud didn't move.

Chaskey slapped his knee and laughed.

"Doan be 'feared, boy. I di'n' come to whup you. Masta

Richard, he doan care no more about you an' me now. He plumb forgot all about us, I 'spec'. So doan you be 'feared."

"I weren't."

Chaskey touched his nose and his ear. "No, I reckon you weren't," he said. "But maybe you should o' bin. Masta Richard like t' beat me to death fo' not killin' you. But you back from Sheol. Reckon Masta Richard be glad to see all the troublies gone outta you. Might even make a good fo'man someday."

Jud didn't know the two blacks in the shanty to which he'd been assigned. They ate, sitting cross-legged, outside it. Two women and another man joined them. Jud tried laughing at a few of their jokes, but it was a hard thing to do. He stopped trying and finished his meal in silence. Blacks were wandering at random; they would join one social knot for a while, and then walk away seeking another. This was the unhurried hour that took place nightly before darkness forced them into their shanties.

Jud walked around awhile and then—for lack of anything better—squatted down and poked at the dirt. He traced a meaningless design with his fingernail. Slowly he obliterated it. At Sheol, he would have been listening to the others, maybe even talking to them. He closed his eyes and listened to their voices inside his head. It was good, but it was not the same.

He walked again. He found Delia, sitting on a stool mending a frock. He sat down opposite her, several feet away. If she was aware of his presence, she gave no indication. He watched her until it grew dark. Then she went into her shanty and closed the door behind her.

AMANDA, THE FOLLOWING AFTERNOON, heard the pounding hoofbeats before anyone else in the Great House; her ears had, after all, been straining to hear the sound for days. She sprang from her chair, crossed the room with little steps so rapid that she seemed to bounce, and pulled open the door, crying, "Richard's home! Richard's come back!"

Samuel sighed, a low elongated sound, the kind a tired man makes at the end of a hard day, knowing that he can sleep now. He had heard nothing, but he did not doubt that Amanda was right; he had never known her to be wrong so far as Richard's return from a trip was concerned.

Samuel pushed himself up from his chair.

Maybelle said, "The hero has come home, having conquered, I'm sure. Now he'll take the burden from you." She patted Samuel's cheek.

Samuel gazed at her blankly. "What burden?"

She had learned not to trust him when he looked thus.

"Why, the plantation, honey. I can see that it's wearing you down something awful having to run it all by yourself." She stroked his shoulder and moved closer to him. He was aware of the odor of the perfume she had dabbed in the cleavage of her breasts. "Poor, tired muscles."

Now they could hear what Amanda had heard, the galloping horse drawing nearer. A couple of blacks were shouting the news.

Samuel looked at her decolletage.

Maybelle smiled, increasing the pressure of her hand on his arm. He did not return her smile. She tried again. Empty moments passed. Her cheeks reddened. She snatched her hand away and spun on her heel.

"Richard's almost here," she said. "We should meet him when he arrives."

"Yes," Samuel said, and now he smiled.

Amanda was standing beneath the portico. Her mouth seemed softer, and her lips were slightly parted. Her small, wide-set eyes were narrowed as she watched the approaching rider.

Richard took his hat off and waved it back and forth over his head as his mount devoured the remaining distance. He reined it to an abrupt halt. The horse danced a few steps, blowing noisily through its nostrils. Its flanks were lathered with sweat.

Richard's face was streaked with dirt. There were dark circles under the armpits of his shirt.

"It's over," he said. "It's all over, as of ten o'clock this morning!"

He tossed the reins to a young black and he dismounted, stiffly.

"My poor baby," Amanda said. She gathered him in her arms. "What have they done to you?"

Richard kissed her. "I'm fine. Really I am. Just fine. Nothing that a bath won't repair."

Samuel recognized the boy's pose, recognized the young animal pride and the desire to be praised. It was justified. The hunt had been hard. Samuel walked forward and extended his hand.

"Welcome home, son."

Richard grasped his hand strongly.

"Was it terribly, terribly difficult, Richie?" asked Maybelle, face half hidden by her fan.

"His name is Richard, dear," said Amanda. "My Richard has never been called Richie since the day I gave birth to him. You do have trouble recalling that, don't you?"

"It seems that I do, doesn't it? But you must remember—" she smiled at Richard "—that *Richard* was such a little boy when I last saw him, that it's very hard for me to think of him as a man now."

Richard dropped his father's hand.

"That's odd," Amanda replied. "You're only a few years older than he yourself."

Maybelle pounced with glee. "I know. I constantly have to remind myself that my dear sister is old enough to be the mother of a full-grown man."

"*Half-sister*," said Amanda.

"Yes. That's so."

Samuel coughed. "Come inside, boy, and tell us what happened."

"Yes," said Amanda, "I want you to tell your mother every little detail."

"Well, some of it is a bit rough." He looked at Maybelle. "You'll stop me if I get too graphic, won't you?"

"Honey, you'll never be *that* graphic. No matter how old you are."

Richard stomped across the porch, opened the door, and held it for her.

"Did you watch over everything while I was gone? Did you keep a close eye on the niggers?"

She brushed past him. "Yes, sweet. A very close eye."

In a dressing gown, while servants were drawing a bath later, Richard slouched casually in a chair, and recounted the event. He and a party of ten had surprised the two remaining fugitives—Shadrach and another—in a barn this morning. The monstrous black had taken three shotgun blasts and two pistol balls before he had gone down. But he'd still managed to kill a planter's son with a pistol shot and two itinerant whites with a sickle. No longer able to stand, he had been set upon by the poor whites in the party, who finished him off with clubs and knives. His body was en route to Olympus. Richard had promised many of the planters that, after the Ackerly slaves had seen it, it would be sent to their plantations, to serve as an example of the consequences of any such actions.

"Thrilling, absolutely thrilling," Maybelle said when Richard finished.

"Quite a job, son," Samuel said.

Amanda leaned forward and patted his knee. "Your mother is very proud of you, dear."

Richard shrugged.

"To think," said Maybelle, "that it only took eleven of you to kill that big black monster. Why, it's as heroic as a Greek myth."

"Why don't you run along and take your bath now, dear," Amanda said.

"Yes, you run along and scrub yourself clean, Richie—Richard. I think I'll go for a little walk."

They left the drawing room. Maybelle paused to examine herself in a mirror. Richard walked up behind her, looking at her reflected visage.

"I thought about you while I was gone."

"Did you now?"

"Yes. Constantly."

Maybelle laughed. "The direct approach didn't get you anywhere, so now you try the indirect, the softer way."

"Why not, Maybelle? What's the matter?"

"Simply," she said, adjusting a comb in her hair, "that I find you repulsive, my sweet."

He spun her around and dug his fingers into her shoulders. "You little bitch! You sashay around looking like you'll give it to anyone old enough to wear pants, but you say I'm repulsive. Why don't you use that mirror to take a really close look at yourself?"

"Let go of me."

"What are you going to do if I don't?"

"I shall scream, Richie. Very loudly."

"Do you really think they'll take your word over mine?"

"I don't honestly know. It would be interesting to find out, wouldn't it?"

"I'll get satisfaction from you. Sooner or later I'll get it." He released her and walked away.

Within the drawing room, Amanda's nostrils were flared. "Samuel," she said, "I do not want that . . . that female in my house any longer."

"What? Amanda, she's your own sister. You—"

"*Half*-sister!"

"All right, half-sister. What has she done?"

"Are you blind? The scandal of her husband taking his own life was bad enough. But on top of that, she has absolutely no shame. I like to die with mortification every time we have a male guest. It's disgusting! And all the time she spends with those niggers. Samuel, it is positively indecent for a white woman to carry on like that, and I won't have it. I will not put up with it a minute longer."

Samuel grasped his chin between thumb and forefinger. "Well, I agree that this business with the niggers has got to stop. I'll speak to her. But as far as leaving the house goes, well, you know that's not possible. It wouldn't be proper for her to go back to her home yet, or to start visiting. Another couple of months, and the mourning period will be over. But until then—"

"She's a damn brazen *hussy,* an' I won't have her!"

When Amanda lost control of her usually precise speech, further discussion was futile.

"I'll talk to her."

"She's goin' to leave, you hear?"

TWO OTHER BLACKS WERE working with Jud when Maybelle came by the carpentry shop. She stopped midway through the door when she saw them, smiled at Jud, and left.

Later, Jud saw that she had captured Plum. They were walking toward a corn crib. The boy kept his eyes cast down, trying to maintain distance between himself and the white woman.

Shadows were lengthening when a stripling set to beating the iron triangle with a bar. The slaves hurried to the meeting shed to answer the summons. There was already a large cluster of blacks by the time Jud arrived. They were *oohing* and *aahing,* and children were crying. Jud heard Richard Ackerly's voice above the commotion.

"Keep moving there," Richard called. "I want every buck,

wench, and child to see this. You all know what he did, and now you can all see what happened to him."

Jud moved up in turn. Hanging by its bound wrists and ankles, slung like a deer or a wild pig on a long pole which was supported by two high sawhorses, was the body of Shadrach. The huge melon-shaped head was thrown back. The eyes were closed, but the mouth gaped open and the purplish and swollen tongue was extended. The face and skull were ripped and bruised. The massive chest was marked with three great rough-edged depressions and numerous punctures and furrows. Much of it was covered with a crust of black dried blood. Fat blue-bottle flies buzzed in lazy circles around the carcass.

Richard caught Jud's eye.

"You're a smart nigger. This could have been you."

Jud gazed down into Shadrach's face. He reached out and laid his palm on the broad cold forehead; then he let his hand fall and moved on.

"Oh, Jesus, no! Oh, sweet Jesus, doan lemme end up like this nigger. No! No!"

Plum fell to his knees before the corpse and wailed. Tears rolled down his cheeks. He rocked back and forth.

"Be my savior, Jesus. Plum love you, Lord! Plum cain't help . . ." He looked around wildly. "I di'n' mean to . . . Oh, Jesus, doan take yo love 'way from Plum. Please, Jesus. Please!"

"Hey, nigger," Richard said. "Stop that. What's the matter with you? Here now, stop that."

Samuel's voice was gentler. "You stand on up now, Plum. Nobody's going to snake a good nigger like you."

Plum wept hysterically.

Jud took Plum by the arm and pulled him up. He led
the boy away. Plum buried his face in his hands and sobbed.
When they neared the shanties, the boy stopped. He stared at
Jud. He whirled and ran off.

Jud looked after him, then went to his shanty for supper.
He worried the ground with a stick as he waited. He thought
about the woman with the yellow turban, his mother. He
thought about Diggs and about Shadrach. And he thought
about Homer. He was sad. He was sad for Plum, too, though
he didn't understand why he included Plum with the others. Richard Ackerly said he, Jud, was a smart nigger. Maybe
he was. Maybe he was a dumb nigger. He didn't want to be
any kind of nigger. He didn't want to be anything. Maybe he
should be with Shadrach and Homer.

He ate alone. He did not want to be alone, but he did not
want to sit with the other slaves either. He finished his meal
and went to look for the girl Delia. He found her where she
had been the previous night. Again he sat down across from
her. He watched her. He felt good.

The fourth night he did this, a fat woman with her frock
hanging about her waist, a baby sucking at one ponderous
breast, walked over to him.

"Hey, nigger, whut you doin'?"

"Nothin'."

"Nothin'? I kin see you ain't doin' nothin'. Jus' sittin'
lookin' at *her*." She pointed. "Like las' night, an' the night before, an' the night before. Whut you want from her?"

Jud didn't answer.

"Well, I goan caution you, nigger, an' you lissen good.
Hear? Mista Samuel ain't bust her, an' Mista Richard ain't

bust her. She still a virgin. Maybe they somethin' wrong wif her. I doan know. But I does know she still got her maidy-head, an' if'n you go pesterin' her, Mista Samuel an' Mista Richard goan cut you up in li'l pieces. So you do all the lookin' you wants, but you keep that dingus of yourn all tucked up safe. You hear?"

Jud nodded. The fat woman looked at him and shook her head.

"Crazy. Bof of you. Crazier 'n loony birds." She waddled away.

THE TOUGH-SKINNED COTTON BOLLS grew larger daily, and several female slaves spent the greater part of their time preparing the raffia baskets and coarse cloth sacks that would be used in the picking. Jud would sometimes lay aside whatever he was working on, walk out of the carpentry shop, and find Delia. He never approached her, and she never acknowledged his presence, but it made him feel good just to see her.

Once he found Richard Ackerly with her. She was re-weaving a damaged basket. Richard was standing behind her. When she reached forward for a shears, Richard slipped both hands under her arms and cupped her breasts. He pressed his loins against her buttocks. She stiffened, then picked up the shears and did the necessary cutting on the basket. Richard said something—loudly and angrily—but Jud was not close enough to hear. Then he stalked away from her. Now that the white man was gone, Jud saw the girl's lower lip quivering.

IT WAS IN THE evening, nearly a week later, that she rose violently from a stool, knocking it over, and marched across the dirt avenue to confront him.

She stood above him with her feet apart and her hands on her hips. "Why you look at me like that, nigger? Why you always search me out an' stare at me like a statue? Whut you want from Delia?"

"I want . . . I don' know."

She frowned and turned to go.

"No," he said quickly. He motioned toward the ground beside him.

She narrowed her eyes. "What for?"

"To . . . talk."

"Talk? Ha! It 'pears to me you cain't say more'n four words."

"You don' have to be 'feared of me."

"Who's 'feared?" She sat down and faced him defiantly.

After a few silent minutes, he reached out to touch her hair. She jerked back.

"I knowed it!" she said. "I knowed certain!"

"No, you don' know. You preten', but you don' know."

"I know Masta Samuel an' Masta Richard, they neither one bring me up to the house yet. But they doan say they doan want me, so no buck better try to pester me."

"I don' want to pester you."

"That all you *do* want." Delia stood up and dusted off her frock. "Keep away from me, nigger."

"Come out and sit with me after dark," Jud said. "Right here. I ain't goin' harm you."

She snorted and walked away.

When the light failed and the yellow glow of lamps appeared in windows, Jud remained seated. The wenching shed was full, and raucous laughter issued from it. Slaves moved about it in the darkness. There were sounds of banjos and music boxes, and a lone harmonica. Slowly, as the hours lengthened, the slave quarters moved into silence, and the lamps were extinguished one by one. A half-moon illuminated the night. Jud waited. Twice he saw a face appear at the window of Delia's shanty, but the door remained closed. When the moon reached its midpoint in the sky, he rose and went to bed.

She did not come out the following night either. Jud waited an hour after darkness had fallen. Then he stood up suddenly, strode across to her shanty, and pounded on the door. He heard only silence within. He pounded again.

"Who that?" asked a suspicious voice.

"Jud."

"You go away, nigger. Go on, git outta here! You leave this wench be, hear?"

"Open up."

"Git outta here, I tell you. You kin stan' there all night an' it ain't goan do you no good."

"You open this door," Jud said quietly, "or I goin' bust it down."

There was no answer.

Jud placed his hands on the door and leaned his weight against it. The clapboard panel sagged and creaked.

"You watchin' this? I jus' playin' with it now. I hardly gots to put my shoulder to it, an' I bust it clean in two. Now, you goin' open up? I ain't goin' wait long."

There was a moment's pause. A wooden latch was worked. The door opened, revealing a tall woman of indefinite age with a sloping forehead. She looked at Jud with desperation.

"Go 'way. Your brains all scrambled. Masta Samuel kill us bof, you do anythin' to this wench. Go 'way!"

Two other women were cowering next to the fireplace. Delia stood alone in the center of the room. She held her head high and looked at Jud through narrowed eyes.

Jud stepped forward.

The woman gave a frightened cry and clawed at his eyes. Jud took her by the shoulder and held her at arm's length.

"Wait!" It was a clear and sharp command from Delia.

Everyone looked at the girl. She drew the silence out, holding them, and then when the first uneasy shuffle came, she said, "Delia go with him."

"Not wif this rutty buck," said the tall woman. "He—"

"Everythin' be all right," Delia said. "You kin watch from the window. Well," she said to Jud, "is you the new door? Cain't you move lessen you pushed?"

Jud led her outside into the darkness. She stared at him, mouth curved down in that remote expression he had seen her wear so often. He met her gaze directly. Gradually he began to wear her down; he saw small muscles twitching around her eyes. She looked away. He averted his eyes a moment or two later, and when he looked back she was toying with her fingers.

Jud did not know what had just happened—but it did not make him feel good.

"You *are* crazy. Or jus' maybe simple," she said.

Jud wanted to say something, but his throat was dry and his tongue thick and clumsy. He could not think of any words.

"Well," she said, "I goan sit here an' look at the moon a spell. An' when I done, I goan back inside, an' then I be through with you an' you kin git on back to where you sleep."

"You a eagle."

"Whut?"

"You a eagle."

"Lissen, you crazy nigger. I'se Delia. Delia, hear? I ain't nothin' an' nobody else. You lucky I let you sit here this long with me. But you talk like that, I goan box your ears an' send you runnin'. You nothin' but a simple, crazy nigger."

"A eagle fly higher'n any other bird."

She glared at him. Jud put his index finger in his mouth, pressed the tip against the inside of his cheek, and snapped it out. He had seen others do it. It was supposed to make a noise. It didn't. He tried again, blowing up his cheeks, and when the finger pulled free it made a popping sound.

Delia's eyebrows bunched together.

He did it again.

Her mouth trembled.

Pop-pop! Twice more, in quick succession.

Delia's lips pulled back from her teeth. Jud grinned. Delia's smile became full. She giggled, and then she laughed. Jud laughed. And their laughter itself became a source of further laughter. Delia clutched her sides. Tears rolled down her cheeks, and she struggled for breath. At length they exhausted themselves, and Jud flung himself on his back, cushioning his head with his hands.

"You a *young* eagle," he said.

"I'm more'n fourteen," she asserted. "An' you ain't hardly but a striplin' yourse'f."

"But you ain't all eagle. You—lemme see—you part, uh, whippoorwill. That it, whippoorwill."

"I declare. You perplexes me, nigger. You truly does. Whut you talkin' about?"

"Whut I be, if'n I a animal?"

"You doan make no sense at all."

"Come on, whut I be?"

She touched a finger to her lips.

"A possum?" he prompted.

"No. Oh, no. Not a possum." She made a face.

"A salymander?"

She rolled her eyes in despair over the suggestion. She stared hard at him.

"A bear," she said firmly. "A big huge-y bear that live up on the top of a mountain in a cave all by hisself. An' you own the whole woods, and you stomp aroun' roarin' all day an' swattin' fish outen the streams an' stealin' honey from the bumblybees."

Jud was partly pleased. "But if I lives there all alone, I don' got no one to talk to."

"*Nobody* gots nobody to talk to. Jus' 'cause some animals makes a lot of noise when they together doan mean they talkin' to each other."

"A big huge-y bear," Jud said. "On top a mountain."

They were silent awhile. Jud sat up. He reached forward, gently. She watched his hand approach. Her lips drew into a thin line, and her eyes widened, but she did not pull back.

His fingers touched her hair and stroked it lightly. She shivered and began to edge away from him. He lowered his hand.

She reminded him of a doe he'd once surprised in the woods. The animal had gone rigid. Its ears had twitched. Muscles skittered in its flanks. Jud had silently willed it to stay, not to be afraid, because it was beautiful and he would have stood there all day if only he could have kept it near. But the doe could not bear the tension. It rose into the air with a high leap, seemed barely to touch the ground, and bounded up again. Jud had stood still, listening to it crash through the dim forest.

He did not want Delia to flee thus.

"Come," he said. "I take you back."

He heard a noise from behind her door, and he knew the three women were waiting there. Her composure had returned. Her eyes were proud and disdainful once more.

"I see you again," Jud said.

She answered him over her shoulder. "Maybe. If I feels like it. I let you know."

Jud went out past the stables and lay down on the grass close to a maple tree. He looked up at the stars. He clenched and unclenched his fists. He could not find a comfortable position. He sensed the great emptiness that lay between him and the stars. It had been some time since he had felt the pull of that emptiness, the deep yearning to flow into it, to be dissolved and drawn forth, rocked in darkness . . . .

The longing was greater than it had ever been before, but simultaneously there was something tight and restraining within him. It blocked his way to the emptiness, anchoring him to the earth, no matter how he ached for the darkness.

When he finally rose, he did so wearily, and he walked back to the slave quarters with heavy footsteps.

He would not have noticed the kneeling figure had it not been for the low sobs. He searched the moonlit ground with his eyes, and found nothing; then he peered into the shadow of a dairy shed and saw Plum. He was about to turn and take another route when the muted voice whimpered to the night.

"Please," Plum said. "Please, sweet Jesus, it ain't my faul'. I tries ever' way I knows to keep outta the demon's way. But it jus' ain't no good, Lord. I gets found an' forced into sin. You knows that true, Lord. You sees it from yo' golden throne. Oh, doan take yo' love from me!"

"Plum?"

Plum screeched, threw himself forward, and curled into a tight ball, knees drawn up to his chin, arms shielding his head.

"No! No!"

"Plum. Plum! It me, Jud. Whut the matter, boy? Whut you 'feared of?"

The boy rolled violently. "No! You cain't take me!"

Jud pinned his shoulders down. "It me, I tell you. Jud. No one goin' take you noplace. Plum, it me, Jud. Now stop that."

Plum opened his eyes. His chest was heaving.

"Jud," he said dully. "Jud. Hu-hu. It my fren'. My fren' Jud. Hu. Hu-hu." He laughed hysterically. "Jud. Hu-ha. Ha-ha-ha. Jud. Jus' an ol' black nigger. Oh, that funny. Hu-hu. That like to kill me it so funny!"

Then he buried his face in Jud's chest, and his arms wrapped around Jud, holding him tightly, and his laughter broke into ragged sobs.

Jud patted him on the head. "Hey, now. Whut put the terrors in you, huh? Whut is it? It all right now, Plum. You safe."

"I thought you the devil. Comin' to spear me wif his pitchfork an' carry me down to the roastin' fires."

"Why you think a thing like that? How come the ol' devil be huntin' you, the goodes' nigger for a hunnert miles?"

"Jud, if'n I ask you somethin', you answer me true, won't you?"

"Course."

Plum gnawed his lip. "S'pose a nigger that love Jesus wif all his heart done somethin' wrong. The absolute wronges' thing. But s'pose he di'n' have no choice, he gots *made* to do it. You think Jesus goan take his love 'way from that nigger? You think that, Jud?"

Jud scratched his head. "Plum, I ain't knowin' much 'bout preachin' an' such things."

"But whut you think, Jud? You reckon Jesus goan punish that nigger, goan punish him terrible? Tell me, Jud. Whut Jesus goan do?"

"Well, I don' 'zackly know. But it seem to me that Jesus goin' unnerstan' that nigger, that he still goin' watch ovuh him."

"You truly does?"

Jud nodded.

"You wouldn't jus' say that?"

"No."

Plum's shoulders slumped. "I bin prayin', I bin prayin' hard as I kin." He looked away. "You know, it writ in the Bible that "'Vengeance is mine,' saith the Lord.' An' 'His wrath'—that mean whut he do when he angry—'is terrible an' quick.' He punish sinners, he punish 'em bad."

Plum said no more for a while. Jud saw thin wet lines roll from his eyes down his cheeks.

"Lemme be," Plum said. "Lemme be. I gots to pray."

EARLY THE NEXT MORNING, excitement knifed through Olympus. The first cotton had appeared. There were haphazard, stunning bursts of pure white fiber, harbingers of the white sea that would inundate the fields in the coming weeks. Children were organized into picking gangs and they trooped out to the fields, dragging baskets and sacks behind them. The older blacks would be held in reserve until it was time for the heavy plant-by-plant picking.

By midday the first sacks were lugged into the square-timbered gin house and emptied into the feeding bins. The gears turned and the hooked cylinders, flat metal ribs, and doffing brushes separated the lint from the hard seeds. Later, cotton would be stored in huge lofts to dry before being fed into the gin, but there was a certain status attached to getting at least a few bales to the market early, so the first day's picking went directly to the hoppers.

Jud was sharpening a saw when Samuel burst into the carpentry shop. The white man's face was florid.

"Nigger, what were you doing with that Delia wench last night?"

"Talkin', Masta."

Samuel was momentarily taken aback. "Talking?"

"Yes, suh, talkin'."

"About what?"

"I don' know. Lotsa things, Masta. Animals an' such."

"Nigger, you're young an' you're horny. Maybe I haven't sent you to the wenching shed enough. That Delia hasn't been up to the house yet. If you try anything funny with her, I'll make a wench of *you. Understand?*"

"Yes, suh."

"Good. Very good. You're not a bad nigger. Just make sure you stay that way." Samuel turned to go. "You're going to keep away from that girl now, aren't you?"

"No, suh."

"What?"

Jud set down the saw and file. "I surely ain't goin' pester her, but I likes talkin' to her, Masta. You di'n' tell me not to do that."

Ackerly searched the boy's face. Rebellion had to be somewhere, the planter thought, in the eyes, in the set of the mouth—but he couldn't find it. One faint trace, that was all he needed, and he would have the boy seized, snaked, and sent back to Sheol. Damn! Ackerly had never seen a face as unreadable.

"Yes," he said suddenly. "You talk to her. You talk and you laugh and . . ." He stalked out of the shop muttering. ". . . and you scratch your wool and you roll your eyes and you work your ass off and you tell them all to go to hell for me and you . . ."

The white man walked out of earshot.

THE LEVEL OF COTTON in the storage lofts rose steadily during the following week, and slowly complements of adult blacks were assigned to the fields. Each day, the number of slaves working around the slave quarters dwindled. Maybelle Farrington was seen only infrequently. Occasionally she stopped to see Jud. Twice Jud saw her with Plum in tow. Plum's behavior was becoming erratic, and Jud had seen Samuel looking at Plum with a critical eye. Plum talked to no one, and had taken to leaping and crying out at the slightest unexpected sound.

SAMUEL SPENT LONG HOURS in the fields. Every physically able Negro was pulling the white tufts from the plants from sunup until the light failed. It had been five years since Samuel had driven himself this hard during a harvest. It was the easiest way to stay away from the house, and he was tired enough at day's end that he could get to sleep early. The Great House had become strife-torn. At best, its occupants simmered in controlled hostility, and at worst they chopped at each other with shouts and screams wielded like hand axes. Even Richard and Amanda were at each other's throats. Only Maybelle retained any semblance of normalcy, and even that was deceptive—she was perhaps the deadliest among them, for she did her ripping and her tearing in a soft, honey-smooth voice, her composure rarely disturbed, her smile always ready.

Samuel himself had been sucked into shouting arguments, and that disturbed him deeply. He felt like a man being drawn down into a whirlpool. Never before had he needed to resort to force, or the implied threat of force, to maintain equilibrium.

Richard now spent his days either hunting, sipping mint juleps on the veranda of a neighboring planter's home and returning to Olympus drunk and surly, or patrolling the fields, driving the slaves with harsh and unwarranted discipline.

Of the three, Samuel was not sure which he preferred.

He'd had a violent argument with Richard over the wench Delia. And that dispute with his son, who had avoided him since then, had led to another with Amanda on the following day.

Amanda had cornered him after breakfast, before he had a chance to escape to the fields.

"Why," she demanded without preface, "can you tell me why—just give me one good reason—you told Richard, literally ordered him, that he was not to . . . to . . . *approach* that little red nigger wench? That Delilah, or whatever her name is?"

Samuel stiffened. This was the question he had prevented Richard from asking, the question he had not permitted himself to ask, much less answer.

"Yes," he said.

"Well?"

"Simply because I don't want him to."

"You don't *want* him to?" She raised her arms. "Do you hear him, Lord? Are you witness to my trials? Samuel, I am trying to discuss this in a civilized manner. God knows the shame I feel, the disgust that sours my stomach for having to deal with this at all. Look at me. Look at my humiliation. Me, a woman, forced by her husband and son to discuss their *lusts*. It makes me feel dirty."

Samuel tightened his bootstrap. "Well, force is about the only thing that would make you even admit its existence."

Amanda flushed. "Do you know what men are, Samuel? Do you know what you are?"

"No, Amanda. What?"

"Filthy, degraded, prurient, muck-wallowing animals."

"That may be, Amanda. That may be. But they're honest."

"Honest! All right, show me some of this honesty. Why won't you let Richard have this wench?"

Samuel slapped his boot and stood up. "Because I won't, that's why. That's all there is to it. I told Richard, and I'm telling you: Nobody touches her. Nobody, do you understand?"

"Yes," Amanda said slowly, "I do. So very well."

Her tone unsettled him. "Amanda, now really, this is all rather unimportant, isn't it? I mean this great fuss over one stupid wench. It's time now that Richard should be thinking about a wife any—"

"A *wife?* Richard? Not while I'm— He's still a child. It will be years before he begins thinking about a wife. But you're not going to turn me off the track that easily."

"It's settled," Samuel said, turning toward the door.

"You're purposely tormenting him. Aren't you? Admit it! If you want her, then take her, you pig. But don't torture my Richard this way. You hear?"

Samuel went out of the room. Amanda hurried after him.

"But it's more than that!" she cried suddenly. "There's something perverse about the feeling you have for that wench, isn't there? Something terrible and unnatural."

"Amanda, the house niggers will hear you."

"I don' care!" she screamed. "I don' care if every nigger on the whole damn place hears. You are corrupt and foul. Perverse, hear? Perverse!"

Samuel cocked his fist. "Shut up! Just shut up."

Amanda clutched her throat. "Oh, God in heaven. How deep can a man sink?"

Samuel left her standing there, and slammed the door behind him.

The subject had not been raised again since then.

In the fields, Samuel noted how closely that big buck, Jud, kept to Delia as they worked. And he knew precisely how much time they spent together when not in the fields and how they spent it. He had made it his business to know.

He was of two minds. His first and perhaps strongest impulse was to transfer the buck to one of the other plantations, sell him off, anything. But there was a factor that held that impulse in delicate check. Delia was a proud, fragile little thing, and earlier, the question of her happiness or unhappiness had never entered Samuel's mind; she seemed to be above such feelings. But now there was Jud, and one of the first times Samuel had observed them together, he had seen her laugh. This had startled him. Laugh? *Laugh?* If so, then she could also cry. She could laugh, and she could cry. She could be happy, and she could be unhappy. Something shattered and fell away from his vision of her. She was *not* after all immune to feeling. She was not a creature complete in herself, independent of everything and everyone. He felt a sense of loss, but beneath that a poignant kind of tenderness.

If that buck could make her happy, well then . . . But oh, Christ! She was so beautiful and so fragile, and Samuel . . .

Damn! Goddamn it to hell!

It was too much. It was too much sometimes, and he

would walk away from them through the fields. Stupid. A goddamn gangly nigger wench.

"Nigger wench, nigger wench," he'd mutter, and some of the blacks would look up at him curiously. "Niggers, niggers, niggers . . ."

I'll burn it all to the ground, he thought: fields, house, and everything. I'll burn the whole goddamn thing to the ground!

SAMUEL WAS SITTING AT the edge of a field, back against the bole of a tree, eating the dinner that had been carried out from the house to him in a wicker basket covered with a checked gingham cloth. It was late in the afternoon, and the blacks were gathered in small clusters, eating their pone.

The harvest was well past midpoint, and long open buckboards loaded with wire-wrapped cotton bales left Olympus daily. Samuel was pleased. Even by a conservative estimate, this promised to be one of the finest crops in Olympus's history.

"Suh?"

It was Jud, with Delia.

Looking at them, Samuel felt a twinge of fear.

"Yes?" he said gruffly.

"Masta Samuel, Delia an' me wants your permission to marry up."

Samuel's right hand jerked reflexively to his thigh where, had he been wearing one, his pistol would have been holstered. Several moments passed before he could force himself to say anything, and even then it was only, "*What?*"

"Delia an' me wants to marry."

"Why, the—" Samuel was about to protest that Delia was too young, but the absurdity of the statement stopped him; most wenches already had sucklers by the time they were fourteen.

"Is . . . is that true, girl?"

"It true."

Samuel snorted. "There's no point in that, girl. Marriage isn't necessary for anything you want to do. There'll be plenty of time for that later. Now you just put it out of your head." His voice was harsh; he hoped the girl would be intimidated.

Hoped she would be intimidated? He cursed himself silently. What was wrong with him? God, that sun was hot. All he had to do was say *No*.

"But I wants to get married, suh." She stepped closer to Jud.

"Wench, you don't know what you want. You think about this for a few months, make your mind up; then we'll talk about it again."

"She know her mind, Masta," said Jud. "An' I know her mind. Don' make no difference, today, nex' year, or the nex'."

Again that damned expressionless face. *No*. Just open his mouth and say it, and it would be over. He looked at Delia. His lips formed the word, but he made no sound. Proud little thing. Beautiful little thing . . .

Suddenly a thought occurred to him. He rose abruptly, flung aside a half-eaten chicken leg, and stared at them with hatred. He shielded his eyes against the sun. "Emerald! Dido! Get over here." The women set aside their pone, gathered up the hems of their frocks, and hurried to Samuel's side. "Take this wench back to her shanty," he said, "and strip her down and examine her. If she's still a virgin . . . well, then, bring her back here. If she's not, lock her in, and come and report to me."

"Yes, suh." Emerald took Delia's elbow. They walked off in the direction of the slave quarters.

Samuel glared at Jud a few moments. The white man was acutely aware of his own physical power. He experienced it, weighed it against Jud's big-boned physique.

He clenched his hand into a fist and slowly, evenly, struck the curled edge against the tree. Again, and again.

In half an hour, Emerald and Dido returned with Delia.

"She fine," Emerald said. "Ain't nobody bust her."

Samuel waved them away. There was scorn in Delia's eyes, and it lacerated his heart. Oh, God! Amanda was right. There *was* something perverse about his having come to such a pass with niggers. He pressed the back of his arm to his forehead; his temples were pounding.

"Masta Samuel," Jud said. "Delia an' me wants to marry."

"Goddamn, boy! Don't you know how to say anything else?"

"Tonight, if'n it be all right."

Samuel's shoulders sagged. He massaged the back of his neck. "All right, girl," he said wearily. "If you want this buck, you can have him."

"Thank you, suh." Cold.

He remembered Amanda, years, years ago—a lifetime ago, rushing to her father's arms after he had consented to her marriage to Samuel, kissing him and crying, "Thank you, *Daddy,* thank you!"

"Tha's good," Jud said.

Jesus! Samuel had to stifle a sudden giddiness. It was some kind of unnatural travesty. *They* were validating and approving *him*. Or was he just imagining it? He rubbed the bony ridges above his eyes with the palms of his hands. Was he going mad?

"Go on. Get out of here," he snapped.

Delia stepped close to him. "Thank you, suh," she said softly. Then she and Jud left.

Samuel watched them walk away. His lips formed the words "Thank *you*." Then he ground the tears from his eyes with his knuckles.

The sky was aflame, a deep red-orange, when the ceremony took place. The slaves gathered in front of the meeting shed, and their mood was jovial. Slave weddings weren't encouraged (family attachments added unnecessary strain to the buying and selling of slaves, and occasionally caused resistance to breeding programs), but they were not directly prohibited, and there was usually a lot of merrymaking attached to them. Maybelle and Amanda stood at Samuel's side, Maybelle enjoying herself, Amanda sucking in her cheeks, expressing a vague disapproval of all this licensed roistering. Richard was home—unusual these days—and sober; equally unusual. He kept himself off to the side, hands clasped in front of him, his sharp face immobile, mouth thinned. His bright eyes never once left Delia. Samuel was holding a new broom.

He raised it up. "All right now. Hush up. Hush there, and let's get on with it."

The Negroes quieted and pressed around in a three-quarter circle. "Jud. Delia. Stand before me, both of you."

Samuel gazed at them. The burning remnants of daylight cast a ruddy glow on his cheeks, but it seemed that without that artificial coloring his skin would be pale, even sallow. He appeared at the moment an old and very worn man.

He cleared his throat. "We're gathered here," he said mechanically, "because Jud wants to make a wife of Delia, and Delia wants to make a husband of Jud. Most of you probably know that already. I have given . . . given my permission to this, and I will record it an accomplished act in my records tonight."

He paused, looking around as if he had forgotten his purpose. The silence lengthened.

"Well," said Maybelle, "are we going to do it, or not?"

Samuel looked at her and bobbed his head. "Yes," he said to the assembly. "Yes. There's nothing further to say." He gripped the broom and singled out a black. "You, Phaethon. Hold the other end of this." They held the broom horizontal to, and a foot and a half above, the ground.

"Life is fleeting," Samuel said. "A short leap, in the eye of the Eternal, from dust to dust. May you pass it together."

Jud and Delia joined hands. Delia gathered up her skirt. They took three quick steps and jumped over the broom. When they struck the ground on the other side, the encircling blacks whistled, stamped their feet, and whooped. Samuel relinquished the broom to Phaethon, who would give it to Delia later—a wedding present from the Ackerlys.

Richard caught Delia's eyes as she whirled in Jud's arms. He smiled slightly and made a curt inclination of his head. Then he turned on his heel and walked off.

"Thank the Lord that's over," said Amanda. "There's something sacrilegious about 'marrying' niggers."

Maybelle patted her hair. "I think I'll go kiss the groom."

"*Maybelle!*" Amanda crushed her lace handkerchief in her hand.

"You don't think I should, darling? Well, then, we might as well go back up to the house."

JUD AND DELIA'S SHANTY was small. It contained a plank table, two stools, and a slat bed with a straw mattress.

It was late. A short wick was burning in an oil dish. In the feeble and flickering light, a visitor might have mistaken the dark stain in the center of the mattress, a bag of coarse cloth stuffed with straw, for a shadow.

It had not been very good, this first joining, awkward and reticent, but what was good was that they had lain together afterward, silently, their bodies touching at several points, hesitantly, timorously drawing warmth from each other.

After a while, Jud sat up. He wrapped his arms around his legs and stared at the wall. The great quietude that enfolded him was alien and unknown. Something like it had been when he had listened to the sounds inside his head. But not really the same, for then he had felt as if he . . . weren't. As if the sound were the only thing that existed. This was different. But even now he sensed that something was askance, that there was something deeper . . . .

He started when Delia touched his shoulder. She felt the tension of his muscles, and let her hand rest motionless until the tautness disappeared. Jud leaned his head on his knees. Delia's fingers moved slowly across his back, tracing and retracing the knotted wales. His eyes began to moisten. His vision blurred. Tears spilled from his lids, ran down his cheeks, and wet his knees.

When he turned to Delia, she pulled back at the sight of his tears. He drew her to him and pressed her head to his chest and stroked her hair. Once she tried to pull away from him, but he prevented her, and then she seemed to collapse against him. She made a choked sound against his chest, and then she held him tightly and began to cry.

Outside, a passerby would have sworn that he heard two children weeping, but he would not have been able to tell whether it was in relief, in anger, or in terror.

WHEN THE LAST BALE had been carted out of Olympus, the gins were cleaned and shut down for another year. The subdued sense of urgency that had prevailed over some three months vanished, and in its wake came a vague melancholy. This lasted nearly two weeks; then it too passed and the plantation successfully readjusted itself to the off-season routine.

The character of Olympus's Great House, which had been statically fixed for more than twenty years, was being reshaped, and as each day passed the momentum of the change increased. Richard frequently left in the early afternoon, and when he did, he rarely returned until very late at night and occasionally not until the next day. He often stank of alcohol. There were rumors—not many, and all delicately phrased— that the company he was keeping in town was not the best and that (here the gossiper prefaced her revelation with: "Oh, Amanda, sweet, I simply *can't* understand how this story was *started,* and I wouldn't *dare* repeat it to you if I didn't *know* it was bald-faced slander, but I *knew* you'd want to . . .") he'd been seen in the area by the railroad sidespur. "You know, where 'that' house is located? The one with the red velvet drapes in its windows?" Amanda was furious. Evil-tongued vipers! She knew her Richard had not been himself of late. And she would soon—yes, poor darling! oh, very soon—give him the attention he needed, comfort him with the balm of love as only a mother can. But for the moment, ah, for the moment she must content herself by addressing loving words to him and patting his head. The rest would come later, not too much later, and her feeling of guilt was light.

The task at hand required first attention. Samuel spent little time at the house. He usually passed his mornings wandering through the work areas. He was more silent now than ever, and was endlessly abstracted. He rarely lost his temper with the slaves, but neither did he stop to joke with them or to approve their work. The blacks missed this contact and felt deprived, and it became a kind of reprise when Samuel passed by to scratch one's head and say, "Wonder where Masta is?" He spent long afternoons in the homes of neighboring planters, and he plunged himself into the ferment seething around the impending Presidential conventions. It was clear that Lincoln had strong support and would very possibly capture his party's nomination. Samuel delivered fierce harangues against the man, donated money to the Southern Democrats, and was—as his interest came to the attention of politically active friends—drawn ever deeper into the cause. And as Samuel's detachment from Olympus grew, Amanda set about entrenching herself as mistress and regent. She gained ground, fortified her position, lunged ahead again . . . .

JUD WAS WORKING ALONE in the carriage house, stripped to the waist, running with sweat. The rear axle of a surrey rested on a sawhorse. He had removed the right wheel with its two cracked spokes and was now forcing the hub of a new one onto the axle, working with a ten-pound sledge against a backing board.

"My, my," said a voice from the door. "Are you strong enough to do that all by yourself, with no help at all?"

Maybelle was standing in the door, her arms folded beneath her bosom, which forced the swollen mounds of her decolletage into greater prominence.

"Yes, ma'am."

"Why, that's just wonderful." She crossed to him, the silk of her pale green dress rustling softly, and she stood behind him.

Jud was conscious of the mass of the surrey before him and of Maybelle's presence, like a weight, pressing in behind him; he felt pinned between the two.

"What's that door over there?" She pointed.

"Feed-bag cabinet." He struck hard with the sledge.

"And that one?"

"Harness room, ma'am."

"Why don't you show me the harness room, Jud?"

"Ma'am, I s'pose' to get this wheel—"

"Jud." Snapped out. A white voice.

Jud set down the sledge and rose to his feet. "Yes, ma'am."

"Oh, yes, you are a tall boy, aren't you?" Her voice was soft again.

Jud led her to the harness room, pushed open the door, and stepped to the side. It was a chamber of moderate size, eight feet square, and harnesses were hung on pegs around the walls in orderly rows. There was a workbench along one wall, littered with strips of leather, brass studs, and jars of grease. Maybelle stepped inside. Her lips pulled back from her teeth.

"Come in, Jud."

"Ma'am—"

"Yes? Now you don't want me to get nasty with you, do you? I'd hate that. Mistreating such a beautiful, beautiful boy?"

Jud stepped inside.

"Close the door," Maybelle said, "and move that crate in front of it." Her voice had taken on a breathy quality. He did. She said, "Come here."

He stood before her, looking down at her. She laughed.

"Like a piece of stone," she said. "Tell me, does the stone ever crack, ever crumble?" She did not wait for an answer. "I never had a chance to—kiss the groom. You know what I want, don't you?"

Jud said nothing.

She turned her back to him. "Unbutton me," she said.

"No," he said.

"Jud," she said softly, without turning. "Do you want to die? You told me once you weren't afraid of anything. Well, I believe you. But you will die, Jud, if I say so, and you know what that means? They take you away from that little girl of yours. Now, maybe she doesn't mean anything to you either. Maybe nothing means anything to you. But if that's true, then there isn't a single reason why you shouldn't unbutton me, is there? And if it's not true, then there's a very good reason for you to do it, because you'll die if you don't. I don't care why you do it, Jud. But do it."

Big huge-y bear. Sometimes she cries. Sometimes she laughs. The white woman says die. Jud's hands moved up; his fingers touched the first button, and then fell away again.

"Jud." Maybelle was breathing heavily. "I'll tell them you tried to rape me, and you'll die. You're not the only one, Jud. Your friend Plum, and Nate—the one with the big shoulders—they've done it, too. Now hurry, Jud."

Jud did what she bade him. She slipped the dress over her head and hung it on a harness hook.

"Spread that piece of canvas on the floor," she ordered.

He stared at the numerous and complex garments that still wrapped her body. She divested herself of the rest of her clothes quickly and unaided. Then she stood naked before him, her loosened hair brushing her shoulders, her hands on her hips.

"Do you like naked white women? Do you like me naked? Take off your pants and let me see if you like it."

When they were on the floor, she said, "No, don't lean your weight on your elbows. On me. On me. Crush me, you big nigger. Break my bones. Oh. Oh, you dead nigger. Harder. Harder, goddamn you!"

She grunted; she twisted under him. And he could see her. White. White. All white. A white woman. White. They were all white. White. He ground his teeth together and the agony of his jaw muscles pounded in his brain. White. White!

He thrust his hips forward savagely.

"Oh!" Maybelle's mouth gaped and her eyes widened.

Kill the white man! It was Shadrach's voice, thundering in his mind.

Maybelle clutched his buttocks. "Oh! Oh! Great black nigger. Black. Nigger. Hurt me. Hurt me. Nigger! Rip me. Hurt me!"

"Yes!" she cried.

White! He hammered at her body.

"Oh, God, yes. Nigger. Nigger. You're hurting me. Hurting me! Yes. Don't stop. Yes! Oh, Christ, *kill me!*"

JUD AVOIDED ALL WHITES. Neither Samuel nor Richard visited the slave quarters much these days, so with them it was a small problem, easily solved by stepping around a corner, or entering a shed. He had little contact in the ordinary course of things with the overseer, and this he pared down with the same simple evasive tactics. Amanda, of course, rarely came near the quarters. Although he distrusted Maybelle, he was not really afraid of her, but something had possessed him that day in the carriage shed that *did* frighten him, and he had not been able to shake it loose. He would smother it, kill it, and let the corpse shrivel and blow away—he had to—but it would take time, and in the interim he knew that he must keep his contact with whites to a minimum.

Despite his efforts, Maybelle sought him out twice again. The first time, what had broken to the surface within him grew stronger. The second time, she cornered him as he was emerging from the smithy.

"You've been avoiding me," she said. "Well, it won't be necessary anymore . . . I'll leave you alone. You see, it's really a very funny situation. I want to be . . . oh, I don't know; I want to be hurt, killed, or something equally ridiculous, I suppose. But I'm also—" She laughed. "I'm also a coward. Isn't that hilarious? The others, they're just right. They're fine. But you, you're really capable . . ." She took an unconscious step backward. "You really *would* kill me."

She turned and walked rapidly away from him.

Jud watched her go. He shied away from what she had said, as a horse would shy away from a snake.

Kill the white man! Shadrach screamed in his mind.

He breathed deeply, and tried with a massive effort to strangle Shadrach's voice. *You live on top of a mountain,* Delia said. Yes, he wanted to live there. With her, the two of them. All alone—surrounded by the thick green forest, and the silence of the woods that was not really silence, but a low, constant murmuring of growth and of small creatures moving quietly, moving softly . . . He worked dully through the rest of the morning. In the late afternoon, he chewed his dinner without tasting it, and as he was finishing, the tension tore through the blanket he had thrown over his mind and drove him to his feet. He walked away from the slave quarters, past the stables, and broke into a run. He ran through the orchards and across the stubbled fields. He pushed himself harder, harder, until he was gasping and his motions were ragged and puppetlike. He stumbled the remaining distance to the edge of the woods, and there fell heavily to the ground.

He lay face down until his heart had stopped thudding and his breathing had calmed. But even then it was still not over. He stood and walked a little way into the forest. He found a long, stout branch. He weighed it in his hands. He cocked it back chest-high, and swung it with all of his strength at a tree. When it struck and broke—the free end spinning off into the brush—he roared at whatever creatures were within hearing distance.

The end slipped from his hands and fell to the earth. He looked down at it without any expression; then he left the woods and started back, walking.

IN THE EVENING, AS Jud whittled a stool leg, Delia moved the oil lamp to the table. She took a paper from beneath a tin plate on the shelf and spread it flat on the table next to the lamp. She sat down, braced her forehead on her hands, and stared at it. She frowned, squinted her eyes, pursed and un-pursed her lips, scratched her head, and made annoyed little sounds in her throat.

"What you got there?" Jud said.

"I doan know. A paper with writin'. I tryin' t' puzzle the words, but it jus' doan look no differen' from chicken scratch-es."

"Here, let's see if I kin sense it out."

"It won' make no more sense t' you 'n it do to me."

"Maybe." He stood behind her and peered over her shoulder. "I kin read some."

"Ha! Where you learn that?"

"When I live at Cap'n Tiligman's."

"Well, if you kin, how come you never say so before? Tell me that."

"Ain't no good for a nigger. Lotta white people don' like niggers t' git smart. I seen one get a finger lopped off for practicin' writin'. But hush now, an' lemme study it."

It was a half-sheet of paper:

Nov 21 1859

    This is Sperry. Michael Redmans nigger. He has leave to visit hiz wife at Olympus. Sameul Ackerlys Plantation. He is ~~tobe~~ to be home before sunup tomorow (Nov 22 1859).

Michael

Redman Esq.

"It a pass," Jud announced after a few moments. "Where you get it?"

"I found it on the ground this morning."

"That skinny nigger—the one who come from Silver Pine—lost it most likely."

"How you know it a pass?"

"That what it say."

"Where?" Delia demanded.

Jud pointed. "That the nigger's name. Sperry. And that his owner's name. Mista Redman. And this say he kin visit his wife here. But he got to be back home 'fore the sun come up."

"Ha!" Delia pushed the pass away. "You makin' it all up."

"No. That what it say."

Delia drummed her fingers on the table; then she became engrossed in cleaning grime from beneath her nails.

"I kin teach you if'n you want," Jud said. "It take a long time, but I kin teach you."

"Who wants to read? It jus' a waste o' time."

Jud went back to the stool leg.

Delia retrieved the pass and examined it again with a frown. "All right," she said suddenly. "If you so smart, let's see if you kin teach me. Let's jus' see."

AMANDA WAS SHOCKED. IT was well past midnight when Ellen, her personal servant, fearfully awakened her and told her that Richard was downstairs—with the sheriff. Amanda came awake immediately.

"What is it? What's wrong?"

"I doan know, Mist'ess. They doan tell me. Hector jus' say, 'Go run wake up Mist'ess 'Manda.'"

The hall at the bottom of the stairs was illuminated by four tall candles. Hector had lighted them, and then had sensibly withdrawn. Ellen, too, seemed to vanish as soon as she had seen her mistress safely down the stairs.

Richard was leaning against the wall, eyes half closed and puffy-lidded, lips swollen and parted. He was singing an obscene ditty to himself. There were four long scratches on his cheek. The sheriff, a paunchy middle-aged man, held his hat by its brim and rotated it nervously.

"Evenin', Miz' Ackerly. Uh, I di'n' think, uh, that is, I thought maybe Mista Ackerly—"

Amanda cut him short with a wave of her hand. "Come to the point, man. What is it?"

"Oh, it weren't really so much, I guess. Jus' a kind of ruckus I had to— Oh, it's all ovuh, nothin' serious. But Mista Richard here, I figured he was too, uh, well, he seemed a bit out of sorts, so I thought I'd best ride back with him."

"Thank you."

He nodded. "Well, I'd best be gittin' back. Evenin', Miz' Ackerly."

"Good evening."

When he left, Amanda took Richard by the arm and led him into the sitting room.

"Stop that filthy singing," she commanded.

She directed him to a chair and drew up another beside him.

"Now what was this all about? The sheriff did not bring you home just to be polite."

"Yes, he did. Oh, yes he did, indeed. A most refined and courteous man, our sheriff. You should invite his wife to some of these afternoon tete-a-tetes and tea gatherings you've been having. Charming man. Charming woman."

"Don't be sarcastic, Richard."

He raised his arm. "The King is dead. Long live the Queen."

"What is that supposed to mean?"

"I don't know. I don't care. I don't give a goddamn who reigns."

"Richard, I've had enough of this. I want to know precisely what happened tonight. If there are going to be repercussions against this house, I want to be prepared."

"No repercush—repre—*repercussions,* Mother. But some juicy gossip, I imagine. All right, sweetie, I'll tell you what little Richie was up to. Do you know Maggie's? Of course you do. Everybody knows Maggie's. Don't look so blank. Maggie's, Mumsy. M-a-g-g-i-e-s. The house by the railroad spur, where those lovely young women reside—all of good families, I assure you, even disenfranchised royalty, some of 'em. Well, as I often am, I was there tonight, consuming great quantities of champagne and being ministered to by one of Maggie's royal trollops.

"But I had too much champagne, Mumsy, and something ... happened. To shorten a long unpleasant tale, I wound up dragging said royal trollop by her hair through the main street of town, beating her, I am told, with truly marvelous vehemence. Well, Mother, how does that strike you?"

Amanda sat straight-backed. "Richard, what is wrong?"

"Wrong? *Wrong?*" He broke into peals of laughter. "Mother, what is *right?*"

"Oh, Richard. Richard. My Richard." She took his hand.

He went down on his knees before her. She took his head between her hands and guided it to her lap. She laid one hand on his neck, and softly ran the fingers of her other hand through his dark hair.

"Richard, I'm sorry. Mother is sorry. It is her fault, not yours."

He began to cry—short, whimpering sobs.

"Mother has been so busy," Amanda continued. "She was wrong. She neglected her Richard. But now she knows, and things will change. She'll make it up to you, you will see."

Richard's voice was muffled by the folds of her skirt: "No ... no ... you don't understand .... No ..."

"Hush, now. Hush, dear. Mother knows. Mother will take care of everything."

He soon fell asleep, an exhausted and drunken sleep, she supposed, for it was troubled, marked with tiny hoarse cries and twitches. She continued to stroke his hair and his cheek.

"There, there. It's all over now. Sleep, my little darling. Sleep."

She was troubled. Without Richard, nothing was of value. It was all for him. Everything. She was nearly finished. It would be different now. She glanced up at the ceiling. The King *was* dead, but he didn't quite know it. He still clung tenaciously to his silly politics, but he had abdicated from all areas of real significance, and soon the realization of that would come upon him. Amanda had what she wanted, and now she could turn her attention once again to Richard. She *had* neglected him, she knew, and she regretted this. But she would rectify that. And perhaps a wife for the boy. Docile, not overly pretty; one who would be grateful for being allowed into the Ackerly family, who would remain in her place. Well, in a year or so she would begin looking for a suitable girl. But time enough for that later. Fortunately, Maybelle would be leaving in three weeks or so. In retrospect, Amanda was glad that Samuel had prevented her from throwing Maybelle out. The incident in town tonight would be no more than a minor scandal; after all, the girl was simply a cheap slut. But to have sent one's own flesh and blood packing would have set tongues to wagging for months. Now all was proper. Richard's humor, Amanda was sure, would take a marked turn for the better once Maybelle left, though why she should dislike Richard so very much Amanda did not understand. And Richard, she knew, was very sensitive to Maybelle's barbs. Just how or why Maybelle could upset him so terribly was beyond Amanda. The important thing was that she did have the power. Well, in just a few short weeks Maybelle would be gone, and that would be the end of that.

Ah, Richard! Richard, my baby. She gazed down at him with tears in her eyes. It was the curse of every mother that no son would ever truly know the unfathomable depth of her love or how very much she had done for him.

She raised his head softly and she bent over and she kissed him on the lips.

Oh, Richard!

THE FIELDS AND SLAVE quarters were silent. Richard had supervised the work four days running, and the leather strap in his hand was frequently and savagely applied. When Samuel had made the rounds, his only interest had been the total amount of work accomplished in a given period of, say, a week. So long as that was satisfactory, he was not upset to discover a knot of blacks idly joking together in the corner of a shed, or a slave taking a little time to lounge in the sun. For nearly three months the slaves had not been supervised by anyone but the rather easygoing overseer and their own foremen. Their labors had not really diminished, but they'd begun to perform them with a certain casualness. Richard brought this to an abrupt halt.

Jud stayed out of Richard's way as best he could. He had pushed Maybelle's words to the bottom of his mind, but he had not forgotten them. The presence of the overseer, who was a fair man and never beat a nigger unless the nigger deserved it, made Jud uneasy. And with Richard, the feeling was greatly intensified. Richard seemed barely to recognize Jud. It was as if single blacks were only components of one big hulking creature called *nigger*, which Richard wanted to control. His concern was to make it perform like some monstrous and clumsy pachyderm, to make it drop to its knees and lower its great head to the dust.

It was evening, and the slaves were eating their supper. Jud was just finishing his dinner when there came a loud pounding on the door. He opened it.

"Have you seen Mrs. Farrington?" Richard snapped.

Apprehension rose in Jud, but vanished when he realized that his was one of the first shanties in the quarter and it was logical for Richard to stop here if he thought any of the slaves could tell him where Maybelle was.

"No, suh."

Richard spat. "Goddamn it." A boy was passing by with a bucket of water. "You there," Richard called.

"Yes, suh?"

"Have you seen Mrs. Farrington?"

"Yes, suh, Masta. L'il while back. By the corn crib near the stable."

Richard hurried away.

Jud closed the door and returned to the table. He chewed slowly, thoughtfully. He finished, and he went to stand by the window. He had been there only a minute or so when he saw Richard returning from the stables. He walked with long, quick strides, eyes fixed directly ahead, face ashen save for two fever-bright circles of red high on his cheeks.

Jud remained by the window. Shortly, he saw Richard coming back from the Great House with Samuel and Amanda. Their faces were grim, but Richard's was sheened with excitement.

Jud pressed his knuckles against the unfinished wood of

the window frame and ground them until they hurt. Then he went to the door, pulled it open.

"Where you goan?" Delia asked.

"There goin' to be trouble."

"Whut kind o' trouble? How you know?"

A few other blacks had seen the Ackerlys pass. A handful had, like Jud, emerged from their shanties and now stood looking at the receding backs of the whites.

"Maybe you best stay here," Jud said.

He closed the door behind himself and began to walk toward the stables. Several other men followed him cautiously.

From behind the stables—where there was a large corn crib—came a shout, then a woman's scream. These were immediately followed by a terrified shriek of undetermined gender.

The slaves huddled close together and rounded the corner that obscured their vision of the corn crib. Behind them, timorous and fearful, more slaves were approaching.

"You goddamn black bastard! You goddamn animal nigger!" Richard flung Plum, who was naked, to the ground and kicked at his head, his genitals.

Plum rolled in the dirt and tried to protect himself. "Oh, Jesus!" he shrieked. "My God an' my Lord. Save me. Save me!"

Maybelle stood off to the side, naked, clutching her dress in front of her.

The door to the corn crib was open.

Amanda's first reaction had been: *Hide it. Let no one know.* But then a moment later, as Richard pulled their nude bodies apart and hurled them through the door, where they stumbled into the light, she realized that this was impossible.

There was only one way to extricate herself from this hideous and ruinous scandal—punish Maybelle as she deserved.

"Cover you'self, you slut," she screamed. "Put your dress on!"

Richard gave the wailing Plum a final kick and shouted to two slaves: "Chain him in the stable. Quick now, you nigger bastards, or you'll get the same."

Maybelle pulled her dress down over her head and shoulders. Without her petticoats and hoops it sagged and hung in loose folds around her hips and legs. Her breasts, unrestrained, were full and pendulous beneath the cloth. She rose slightly on the balls of her feet and backed warily away.

Richard lunged and seized her by the wrist. She raked his face with her nails.

"You bitch. You goddamn nigger-fucking slut."

He slapped her, rocking her head. She clawed and kicked at him. He punched her, brought his knee up sharply into her groin, causing her to gasp and bend forward. He pummeled her, slapped her, grabbed savagely at her breasts, all the while screaming in a high-pitched voice, "*Bitch! Bitch!*"

Samuel, looking dazed, dropped a hand heavily on his son's shoulder. "Enough," he said. "That's enough."

Richard was flushed and his long hair hung down from his forehead over his eyes. There was spittle on his lips.

Maybelle glared at him, wiped a hand across her cut and bleeding mouth. She pulled a partly torn strap of her dress back up her shoulder.

Samuel gazed at Maybelle stuporously. "Leave," he said. "Get out."

"Gladly. I'll be gone as soon as I've changed. You can send my things after me."

"Get off this plantation now," Samuel said. "Now! If you're still here in five minutes, I'll . . . I'll *kill* you."

Richard grabbed his father's shirt. "No! You're not just going to let her go. No. She's a pig. She's an animal! She's *lower* than a nigger. She was laying with a nigger, don't you understand? A black nigger. She was naked under that buck. She had him *inside* her. She's foul! She's got to be punished."

"She has dis-*graced* the entire family," Amanda said. "She is worse 'n a scabrous hoor. She must suffer. She must *pay!*" She flew at Maybelle.

Samuel stepped between them.

Richard caught his father's shoulder. "Whip her!" he said. "She was laying with a nigger. A *nigger.* She's got to be snaked!"

"Yes," Amanda cried. "Whip her. Whip her. Just like a nigger! It has to be done. You know that," she insisted.

Samuel nodded dumbly.

Richard dragged Maybelle through the slave quarters, crying: "This is a white nigger. A white nigger! We're going to snake her. We're going to tear her hide off." Slaves poked their heads from doors, stared incredulously, ducked back into their shanties, and emerged only after the whites had passed. They followed at a respectful distance and kept well back when they gathered behind the meeting shed.

Richard flung Maybelle up against the whipping post. She struck it and fell to her knees.

Richard pointed at one of the nearest blacks. "Run to the shed and fetch me the snake. Be spry!"

He pulled Maybelle up. She was dazed. He lashed her wrists together and to the iron ring near the top of the post, stretching her arms above her head, raising her so she could just stand on her toes, and snubbed the end of the robe around a hook.

The slave he'd sent for the whip returned and advanced fearfully, extending his arm. Richard snatched the coiled whip, and the slave scampered away.

"Look, you niggers. Look!" Amanda cried. "I want you all to see. I want you all to know that Amanda Ackerly don' cherish any viper in her home. When they ask you, you tell 'em whut you saw. You tell that your mist'ess *spit* on that she-devil, even though she was her own kin. You tell 'em that your mist'ess di'n' make any exception. She punished that bitch jus' like she'd punish anyone else. You watch, an' you tell 'em whut you saw."

Richard took hold of Maybelle's dress at her shoulders. His fingers trembled.

"You never did get it, did you, Richie sweet?" Maybelle said to him.

He made a choked sound. He clutched at her garment and tore it down to her waist.

He stepped back and slashed the whip across her back.

"Slut!" Amanda shouted. "Harlot!"

"You dried-up old bitch. You don't—"

Richard struck again.

"—*hhmmeh!*"

On the third lash, Maybelle screamed: "You can't hurt me, you little bastard! You can't hur—*hhmmeh!*"

Richard laid into her again. Perspiration streamed down his red cheeks. "Beg!" he yelled. "Beg me to stop!"

The next stroke split the skin across her shoulder blades, and Maybelle jerked at her tether. She gasped, sobbed, and clamped her lips with her teeth until blood appeared at the corners of her mouth. Richard shouted at her to beg, to scream. Her eyes distended each time the whip fell. When the number of crimson liquid lines across her back surpassed the unbroken welts, she began beating her forehead against the post.

"Scream, goddamn you!"

"Bastard," she said, weakly and breathlessly.

But on the next stroke, her high keening scream split the chilly evening air, startled the mesmerized slaves, and made them leap back.

"Yes," Richard said. "Yes." He repeated the word each time the whip struck. Maybelle flung her head back, throwing herself from side to side.

"Stop! Stop it!" she shrieked. "I can't stand it. *Aaiiee!* Stop it! Oh, God! Please, please, oh, *please!*"

Then her body sagged.

"All right," Samuel said, walking up to Richard. "It's over."

Richard lashed Maybelle's unconscious form again. Samuel reached for the whip. Richard pushed him away. "No!"

Samuel wrenched the whip from his hand. "She's still white," he said, "and you can't kill a white person."

"She's just fainted," Richard said. "She's nowhere near killed."

Samuel held the whip from him. "She's not as strong as a nigger, can't take it like a nigger can."

Richard's lower lip was trembling. He was breathing heavily. For a moment, he looked ready to argue.

"Look at her," Samuel said. "Look."

Richard did. Slowly, he calmed. "All right," he said. "I'm satisfied."

"Have her taken into town," Amanda said. "There's a train goes through at ten. Give a nigger some money; have him buy her a ticket and put her on board. But see that he keeps to the back ways, hear? And get her bundled up good so no one recognizes her."

She spun on the Negroes, and a few of them cried out.

"You see what happened to her, niggers? Did you all see it good? Well, that's nothin' next to what'll happen to any one of you who breathes the slightest word about this. Understand?"

Maybelle was loosed from the whipping post and taken to a shed. A slave washed her back down with brine. Maybelle screamed, but did not come fully conscious. She lay on her stomach on a wooden bench, arms hanging down on either side.

"Bastards," she mumbled. "Go to hell . . . go to hell, bastards."

But then, when a girl touched her to help her dress, she winced and began to whimper, and was still whimpering as the buckboard rattled away from Olympus.

Amanda remained in the house after Maybelle was taken away. Richard insisted that what was to follow was not fit for a woman's sensibilities. Amanda did not protest. Maybelle had been the important one anyway, and they were done with her now. For good. The story would leak out. That could not be prevented. But the whites into whose ears the garbled accounts of the blacks finally wound their way would have a hard time determining just how much of it to credit. And it was certain that they would not approach any of the Ackerlys directly. Oh, there would be gossip all right, and plenty of it, but with nothing to feed upon save the original rumors, it would die out soon enough. Amanda didn't need anything more.

THE BLACKS WERE MASSED around the stable in which Plum was chained when Richard and Samuel returned to the slave quarters, waiting silently. Darkness was spreading. Richard ordered torches lit. He had a brazier brought to the slaughterhouse and strips of flat iron inserted in the coals; red-hot metal seared wounds closed, and Richard did not want Plum to bleed to death. He opened the door to the stable. Plum was chained by his ankle to an upright support beam. He was on his knees, eyes closed, hands clasped fervently before his face. He screamed when he saw Richard. He flung himself backward and began jabbering.

Richard freed the end of the chain and pulled it. "Come on, nigger."

"No! No, Masta, suh. She force Plum, Masta. Plum try t' git away. He try, suh. But she make him sin, Masta. She make him. Doan hurt Plum. Doan kill Plum!"

Richard wound the chain around his hand and dragged Plum out. Plum clutched at the ground, trying to stop himself.

"*Please*," he shrieked. "Doan kill me, Masta. Jesus, my God an' my Savior, have mercy on yo' servant! Save me, Jesus, save me!"

They approached the slaughterhouse. The naked wailing black was dragged inside, arcing a stream of urine across the door frame. The congregated blacks pressed in toward the building.

Plum's younger brother, Harris, fell to his knees. His eyes were wide, his jaw hung slackly, and his hands were stretched out in supplication. He moaned. Chaskey lifted the boy to his feet, pressed the child's face into his chest and led him away to a shanty.

Plum was sobbing hysterically from behind the door.

Richard's words came through clearly. "Now you be quick with those irons, hear? When I cut, you seal."

"Yes, suh," answered a deep voice.

"You had a white woman, eh?" Richard said coolly. "You saw her naked with your eyes, you kissed her maybe, too, huh? You put your hands on her white body. And you put— this—inside her."

"Jesus, I love you!" Plum wailed.

Then he screamed.

"There. You're not going to love anybody or anything again. Quick, you. Get that iron down on him. Good. All right, stretch his arms out and hold his hands down here. Tight, goddamn you! Keep him from squirming. Steady now . . . steady now . . . umph!"

Plum screamed again.

"*Fast* with those irons. On the left wrist there. Quick, he's still spraying blood. Shut that screaming up, nigger. Shut up, I say!"

The screaming continued.

"Put him on his back," Richard ordered. "Pry his mouth open wide. Wider. Goddamn it, get your fingers between his teeth. That's it. Now you, Cabe, hand me those shears. Uh-huh. Uh-huh. Keep him still! There—umph! Now sear it. Inside, all the way back! Farther, else he'll drown in his own blood. Cabe! Cabe, where are you going? Oh, goddamn it. Finish it up, Raphe."

Cabe stumbled out through the door. The black's thick forearms glistened with blood. He sagged against the door-jamb and vomited.

And then for a while there was only the sound of Richard's voice and an occasional answer from Raphe. But if the slaves waiting outside strained their ears, they could hear, too, a low and constant *uhhnh . . . uhhnh . . . uhhnh.*

In a short time the door opened and Richard appeared in a sudden flare of torchlight along with Raphe, holding a third figure between them. Beneath his sightless eyes, Plum seemed to be grinning. But one realized an instant later that this was an illusion: that the white expanse of teeth was visible only because the lips were gone. The boy's head rolled on his shoulders. The wound between his legs was charred, as were the stumps in which his wrists ended.

"Oh, sweet Jesus," a woman moaned, "save us all."

The blacks shrank back. Samuel followed, looking tired and abstracted.

"Stop," Richard said.

He took a clasp-knife from his pocket, bent, and hamstrung Plum with two deft strokes. "Throw him down."

Plum struck the ground and rolled to his back. He flopped

there, turned on his stomach again, jackknifed his spine, gained his knees, and then fell to the side. He lay still, going: "*Uhhnh . . . uhhnh . . .*"

"I don't want anyone coming near him," Richard said. "He stays here, just like this, until he's finished." It was not necessary to repeat the warning.

Richard and Samuel left. Slowly the blacks began to break up and return to their shanties.

THE SHANTY WAS DARK. Delia was lying on the bed, but Jud knew from her breathing that she was still awake. He was sitting on the floor, his back braced against the wall, staring at the red glow of the dying embers in the fireplace. In not too great a while dawn would come. He shivered. He was cold, but he did not think to wrap a blanket around his shoulders. He grunted. Several minutes later he grunted again. He rose and crossed the shanty.

He rummaged in the blackness through a raffia basket until his fingers closed about a long iron knitting needle.

"Whut you doin'?" Delia asked as he walked back.

"Nothin'. You go to sleep now."

When he opened the door, she said, "Jud?"

"Hush. We both asleep. We sleeped all night."

"Jud, you goan to him, ain't you?" She sprang from the bed and took him by the shoulder. "You cain't, Jud. You heard whut Mista Richard said. You go near that poor nigger, you git the same thing done to you."

He pushed her gently away. "Quiet, girl. I right here by you—sleepin'." He slipped out and closed the door behind him.

The moon was three-quarters full, and pale, washing the night with sterile light. Jud kept to the shadows. His breath misted before him, and the needle was cold against his skin.

Plum was lying on the open ground, face down, still, looking unreal in the gray light of the moon. Jud paused in the shadows; then he strode directly forward. He knelt at Plum's side and raised the needle. He paused. Then he lowered it. He reached out and felt for the large prominent vein in the throat. Plum's skin was cold. There was no pulse. Jud stood and walked away.

When he returned to the shanty, Delia was sitting in bed crying. He sat down beside her and put his arm around her.

"Hush, now."

She pulled away from him. "They goan kill you. You kilt you'se'f. They goan hang you up an'—"

He put his finger to her lips. "Shhh. Shhh. He dead when I got there. I di'n' do nothin'. It all right. Quiet, now."

She wept against his chest, and he stroked her hair. Soon she was asleep. He eased her down, covered her, and slid from the bed to his pallet on the floor. The bed was not large enough for both of them. He slept at its side on the pallet.

He pulled his cover up to his chin. An hour and a half later, when day broke, he was still staring at the ceiling.

IN THE SPRING, THE Republicans nominated Lincoln.

Samuel raged through the Great House, pounding the fist of one hand into the palm of the other. "The idiots! The morons!"

There were guests that afternoon in the Ackerly drawing

room, three elegantly dressed young men and two demure young ladies along with Richard in the center of the room while Amanda and the mothers of the two girls sat off in a corner, drinking tea from delicate china cups.

As Samuel stormed through the hall on the other side of the closed door, Richard stopped in the middle of a sentence, holding up his thin, long-fingered hand. He listened, then laughed.

"One would think this had been a complete surprise. 'Lincoln? *Lincoln?* Who, by God, is he?'"

An appreciative titter rippled through the room.

Amanda smiled.

Lucille Vickers, a plump and jowly woman whose presence represented her first invitation to one of Amanda's afternoon gatherings and who perched nervously on the edge of her chair and nodded vigorously every time Amanda spoke, leaned at an even more acute angle and whispered: "You have simply a marvelous son, Mrs. Ackerly."

"Why, thank you." Amanda inclined her head toward the hall. "It—oh, how should I say it? It hasn't been the easiest job to raise him properly."

Lucille impulsively took one of Amanda's hands. "And don't for one moment think that everyone doesn't realize that, dear."

Amanda smiled and slipped her hand free. Lucille blushed and sat back.

DELIA'S BELLY WAS SHOWING the first signs of tumescence. At night she and Jud would run their hands over it, bemused smiles on their faces, a giggle breaking from her, a laugh from him. Prima, the knobby-knuckled crone into whose care the sucklers and very young children on Olympus were given, had confirmed Delia's pregnancy a month ago, but neither Jud nor Delia had believed it until the swelling began.

There were changes, mostly in Delia. One night, not long after Plum's death (Plum had been metamorphosed in a short time into a kind of bogeyman—"If'n you doan simmer down, ol' Plum goan come grinnin' up from his grave an' carry you off"), Jud had said: "You know that mountain where the big huge-y bear live? Well, he don' live there alone. He live with a eagle. A eagle that part whippoorwill. That where they should live. That where they belong. On a mountain, all by theyse'ves."

Delia's pink tongue darted over her lips. She glanced at the door. "You shouldn' talk like that. Someone hear, an' 'port you to Mista Richard."

"They nothin' wrong with talkin' 'bout animals, jus' animals. What you think?" he coaxed. "That eagle-y whippoorwill like that mountain much as the ol' bear? It like to live there with jus' the bear an' no other animals?"

"It . . . it prob'ly would. Yes, I thinks it would."

And they talked many nights, close together, voices low, about how it would be on the mountain.

Jud made a quill from a goose feather, and secured scraps of paper from the Great House refuse. He used black dye mixed with a little water for ink. With these he taught Delia a little writing, and he used Samuel's discarded newspapers to teach her reading. She was apt, but easily frustrated, and several times she flung aside the quill and ripped up the paper.

But in a day or two she would ask Jud to sit down with her again.

When her belly began to grow, though, all this stopped. She refused to let him discuss the mountain. She wanted him to throw away the quill and paper. He believed this was only temporary, that it would last no longer than her pregnancy, so he hid the writing implements and held his talk of the mountain in abeyance.

But he did not stop thinking about it. In the fields, chopping out the weeds that competed with the new young cotton plants, he pictured the scene; he knew what kind of trees grew there, knew the density of the underbrush, felt the texture of the leaves and pine needles that carpeted the ground, and heard—actually heard—the silence.

IN THE PERIOD BETWEEN Lincoln's nomination and the blooming of the cotton plants, Samuel spent little time at Olympus. He went on three- and four-day political speaking trips in the company of influential planters. Most of these men dressed in somber clothes and were grave-faced and quiet-spoken. Amanda invited their wives to her afternoon gatherings, and when it became apparent that she would not be put out by hearing the prevailing opinions of her husband, indeed seemed to welcome such information, her guests spoke freely. Samuel, it seemed, was viewed by his associates as a buffoon. He was less than a political neophyte, totally ignorant, but possessed of a certain inexplicable zeal—frenzy was perhaps more appropriate—and thus there was a use for him.

Amanda was content. There was little that she would

change. Oh, those twin sisters, the octoroons that Richard had bought, were an annoyance, it was true, and she definitely did not approve of the way he carried on with them, particularly when he had both of them in his room on the same night. But it was a small thing, really. He had been coming along so nicely lately that Amanda did not have the heart to make an issue over them. And he was, after all, properly discreet about them.

XERXES—THAT WAS THE name sent down from the Great House for him—was born in the final week of the picking season. A stripling brought the message out to the field, and Jud was given an hour to go back and see the child.

Prima was standing outside the shanty. She took his arm and wagged a skeletal finger beneath his nose.

"Look here, you big nigger. The girl had a hard time of it, so doan you go botherin' her none, hear?"

Jud nodded and went inside.

Delia was lying with her eyes half closed, cradling the squalling baby. She smiled sleepily when she saw Jud.

"How you feel?"

"Tired. Pow'ful tired."

"Kin I see him?"

"Careful of him," she said.

He took the child gingerly and peered at it curiously. It was a big baby, but it was dwarfed in his grip. He had little sense of having anything to do with this strange, wrinkled little creature. Any bond between him and it was indirect, through Delia. The child waved its arms and cried.

Instinctively, Jud drew back. "It got good lungs," he said.

"Yes." She took Xerxes from him, nestled him back at her side.

Jud tugged at his ear. "Well, I s'pose I best be goin' back to the field now."

"Yes."

At the door he said, "Sure is a big one." Then he left, feeling helpless and bewildered.

THE HARVEST SEASON WAS only a few weeks past when Lincoln was elected President. Amanda was curious as to how Samuel would receive the news. Following the nomination, the elder Ackerly had campaigned furiously on behalf of John C. Breckinridge—and in June, Breckinridge had captured the Southern Democrats' nomination. That night Samuel had attended a celebration at the home of a neighboring planter. As the story was related the next day to Amanda, Samuel had not drunk much—two, maybe three whiskeys at the most—but from the very beginning he had been boisterous and highly, almost maniacally, euphoric. He'd left the party, alone, a little after one in the morning to return to Olympus. What had occurred between then and dawn, when Hector had found him sitting outside on the bottom step of the veranda, staring at his boots, his untethered and still-saddled horse feeding on the sweet young grass of the lawn, no one could say.

They took him upstairs, undressed him, and put him to bed. He lay there, apparently not hearing anything that was said to him, looking up at the canopy above him. The doctor found neither bruises nor cuts—nothing that would indicate a fall. Nor was there any sign of heart failure or epileptic seizure.

"Frankly," he told Amanda, "I cain't find nothin' more'n a generalized exhaustion. But even that doesn't account for the way he is. The only, uh . . ." He coughed, removed his spectacles, and began to polish them.

"There is something more. I can tell. What is it?" Amanda urged.

"Well . . . You see it now an' again in truly sick people. Appears as if they just don't want to live anymore, an' they give up. Happens sometimes in men his age, too. And—uh—well, this politickin'. Lots of times they git hyperactive just before it sets in. But that happens mostly 'mong poor folk. Never known a case with a man like—" he made a gesture meant to include the whole of Olympus "—Mista Ackerly."

"What can we do?"

"Not awful much, I'm afraid. Let him get some rest. Feed him meat. Then in a while get him up and try to involve him in something."

Amanda often brought Samuel meals herself. She was solicitous, and spoke to him slowly, as if to a child.

"Here, Samuel. Look what I've brought you. I've brought you dinner. Would you like to eat some?"

To the house servants she repeated each week that they were not to do or to say anything that would excite him (the first week she had said, "that would invol— that is, excite him").

Samuel hadn't left the house since that day; indeed, he had spent most of his days in bed. He would listen when someone spoke to him, but rarely did he answer.

Amanda was not really worried about the effect the news would have on him, but she did want to see his reaction.

"Oh, by the way," she said as she fluffed his pillows behind his back, "Lincoln won the election."

He smiled at her; then a moment later he said, "What?"

"Abraham Lincoln was elected President."

"Oh."

Amanda turned away from him; her face was radiant.

ALTHOUGH XERXES HAD BEEN given into Prima's care, Delia visited him several times daily to suckle him. And in the evening she brought him back to the shanty for a while. He was a strong baby, and he grew rapidly. Jud liked the baby because Delia made a great fuss over it and it made her happy. In itself, it still seemed a very strange thing to him.

Shortly after Christmas, the overseer came to Jud's door in the early evening. Jud barely checked himself from closing the door in the white man's face. This unnerved him; he was becoming less and less able to remain in the presence of white people. Other niggers he could tolerate, could successfully ignore. But when a white man was near, there was a tightening in his chest, perspiration broke out on his palms, and his hands clenched involuntarily into fists.

Chaskey and another black stood behind the overseer.

"How your muscles feelin', Jud?" asked the white man.

"All right."

"Good. Come on out here. We got a job to do."

Jud breathed deeply, tried to think about nothing, and stepped outside.

The white man led them across the fields and into the woods, in the direction of the public road.

Chaskey walked loosely and chafed his arms for warmth. "We goan cotch us a nigger-stealer," he said. "You know that peddler that Mista Richard run off today? Well, he tol' Prince here to meet him on the road, by that big ol' gnarly oak. Say he goan take Prince up Norf to freedom. But Prince, he no dumb nigger. He tell."

"He a good nigger all right," said the overseer, pushing through the leafless brush. "Freedom, hell. That ain't no stinkin' abolitionist. He the worse they is. A nigger-stealer. Carry Prince right into Tennessee, an' sell him to a new masta."

Prince spoke for the first time. His voice was high and boyish. "He tell me Souf Car'lina ain't part of the country no more, that it se—that it ses—"

"It secede," said the white man. "That true enough. We all vote on it, withdraw from the Union. Other states gonna follow. We gonna have our own country, the Confederate States of America. But he tell you that just to bait you, boy."

They arrived at the meeting place. The moon was hazy above a layer of clouds, but there was enough light to see the road clearly.

"We got 'bout half a hour," said the overseer. "Now when that man come up, you gonna step out an' meet him, Prince. Us three'll be hidin' here. Just the minute you an' him start off, we leap out an' take him." To Jud and Chaskey he said, "We'd ruther take him alive if'n we can, but they's no need to gentle him. 'Member, this ain't a white man. Not no more, leastwise. It the lowest thing that breathe."

The peddler came walking down the road later, bent under the load of his knapsack, a slouch hat pulled low on his forehead, greatcoat buttoned to his chin. He was humming to himself. He stopped, glanced up and down the road, and gave two short whistles. Jud, Chaskey, and the overseer were crouched a dozen paces away. Prince moved into the open.

"Ah, good nigger," said the peddler. "Right according to schedule. All right, listen good. Your name is Kip. Unnerstan'? Kip. If anyone asks, I bought you in Virginia more'n a year ago. Now, what's your name, where'd I buy you, an' how long you been with me?"

"I Kip, Masta," the boy said. His voice quavered. "You buy me in Virginy 'bout year past."

"Good. But don' be skeered, boy. You got t' look natural. All right, let's get started."

"Now!" the overseer shouted.

Jud and Chaskey sprang forward. The peddler shrugged off his pack with a quick motion, and a length of pipe appeared in his hand.

"Get back, you black bastards," he yelled.

Chaskey lunged at him. The peddler sidestepped and clubbed the slave as he went by. Chaskey sprawled to the ground and didn't move. The peddler pivoted and swung at Jud. Jud deflected the pipe, receiving a grazing blow on the forearm. His hands closed about the white man's throat. The peddler brought his knee up into Jud's groin. Jud's fingers slipped loose and he doubled over.

The overseer was standing to the side, his hand on his holstered pistol. He did not want to use the weapon unless forced to.

The peddler's arm rose for another blow. Jud caught his wrist and seized his elbow with his other hand. He and the peddler stared into each other's faces. Then slowly, steadily, Jud increased the pressure. The white man's eyes widened. He made one last effort; then he gasped and dropped the pipe.

"You got him, boy," the overseer said.

The peddler's shoulders slumped. He waited for Jud to release him. Jud bore down harder on his arm. The white man looked at him with a startled expression that quickly melted into panic. He screamed and tried to jerk loose. Jud grunted.

The peddler's elbow socket was torn apart with a snap.

Jud drove his fist into the peddler's mouth, pulping the lips and splintering teeth.

"Jud, that's enough!" the overseer yelled.

Jud hammered at the peddler's body; he hit him again in the face and cracked his jaw.

"Jud!"

The peddler collapsed. Jud caught him before he struck the ground, caught him by the throat and the crotch, and lifted him into the air.

"*Jud!*" The overseer stood before him, pistol in hand. "Put him down."

Jud paused, the unconscious peddler still suspended above his head.

"Put him down, I tell you!"

Jud lowered the peddler, laid him on the ground, and stood staring off into the woods, face blank.

"Goddamn, boy," said the overseer, kneeling at the peddler's side. "He gotta go into town for trial. You come close to killin' him, you know that?"

Jud said nothing.

The overseer looked up. "Whut got into you, boy? You acted like a wild . . . Whut's wrong with you, nigger?"

"Nothin," Jud said abruptly. He walked over to help Chaskey.

AFTER THE SPRING RAINS had gone, and when the first tiny buds had appeared on the trees, Samuel rose from bed one morning and politely asked one of the house servants to help him dress to go outdoors. He wandered awhile, hesitantly, like a child in a strange place, through the slave quarters. The blacks were astonished by his pallor, by the way his compact body had grown flaccid and soft, and by the uncomprehending placidity in his eyes. They greeted him unsurely.

Samuel nodded at them, and smiled.

Later he left the quarters and walked over the grounds in front of the Great House, sitting down at last on a marble bench set in an arbor whose vines were still bare and therefore did not obscure his vision. He sat quite still, with his hands folded in his lap. He looked up at the portico, the tall pillars, and the gleaming white height of the Great House. And in his mind the sky around him darkened; it became night, and the house was illuminated by the moon. A muscle fluttered in his cheek. His body began to sway, as it had swayed with the motion of the horse the night he had galloped back to Olympus from the party celebrating Breckinridge's nomination. He left the public road, spurring his mount beneath the arch and through the stand of oaks; then he left the trees, the rolling lawn and the gardens and the ponds and the arbors, and the huge house itself with its darkened windows exploded in his vision. Without realizing it, he tightened his grip on the reins, slowing the horse somewhat. The night was quiet. Nothing moved. And as he drew nearer the house, it seemed as if the entire scene were a fantasy, some sort of lifeless shadow of a reality long ago destroyed. Fear rose within him, and he forced his horse down into a slow trot. It was not real; it was a facade, a painted canvas beyond which lurked something terrifying. He laughed brittlely and shook his head. Fool, you're overtired, drunk maybe. Breckinridge. The campaign. It is real. It is. Real? Breckinridge? The last few months? What did all that have to do with him? Him, Samuel Ackerly. What did it mean to him? Nothing. Not a goddamn thing. What concerned him was here. Olympus. This was where he was, where he belonged. But look. Look. There was nothing there. It was illusory, all of it. It was gone! What he saw did not really exist; it was only some sort of horrible trap that had been set for him. Everything he touched would crumble to dust. He would be devoured. The horse had now slowed to a walk. He wanted to stop it, but could not. He wanted to turn and flee. But whatever it was that was crouching before him, it was drawing him closer . . . closer . . . . It was irresistible . . . inevitable . . . . There was no escape! . . . Everything was disintegrating around him . . . everything . . . .

In the arbor, Samuel gave a hoarse little cry. He pulled his arms into his sides and hunched over as if in pain. He buried his face in his hands.

There was . . . something . . . something. There, it was slipping away. Better. Better now.

He raised his head. The sun felt warm upon his back. His face was tranquil, and he was smiling.

NED PEARSALL SAT LOOSELY in the saddle of his standing mount and sucked thoughtfully on the stem of his pipe. He was a young man, with fair hair riffled by the breeze. Looking down the center avenue of the shanties, he said: "You surely have an effective system here, Richard. Everything neat and streamlined. Hardly any wastage that I can see."

"It took a bit of doing, but it runs pretty smoothly now."

To their right, in front of the large shanty in which Prima watched over the sucklers and young striplings, a baby began to bawl. It was late afternoon and several wenches were visiting their offspring.

Richard's pipe went out. He cupped his hand to shield the bowl from the wind as he relit it.

"They have no right to occupy a fort in our harbor," Ned said, picking up their conversation of minutes ago. His horse did a nervous sidestep. He patted its neck. "Easy, Hook, easy."

"Why, how the hell," he continued, "do you think they'd take it if we sailed a gunboat up the Potomac and—hey!"

Hook tossed his head and whickered. A fat naked baby was crawling toward the horse.

"Whoa there, Hook. Stand easy."

The horse whinnied and stamped the ground. The baby looked up and howled in fright. At the sound the horse reared, stood on its hind legs, and pawed the air.

"Easy, damn you, easy!" Ned swatted the animal's ears and tried to wrench its head to the side.

The baby screamed. Hook's flailing hooves plunged down. Ned leaped from the saddle.

"Oh, hell!" He grabbed the reins and lashed Hook across the face. "Damn spooky horse!"

"*Xerxes!*"

Delia ran from Prima's side, scooped up her battered baby and clasped it to her breast. "*Xerxes!*"

Ned passed Hook's reins to a black and he reached out for the baby. "Here, let me see."

Delia hugged the baby tight to herself.

"Don't be hysterical. Give it here." His hand touched a thick substance oozing from the cracked skull. "Oh," he said. "Oh. I'm sorry. It's . . . what can I say?"

Delia's eyes went wide. She stared at Xerxes, shaking her head from side to side.

Richard dismounted and came to Ned's side. Ned said, "Damn, I'm sorry, Richard." He looked furiously at Hook. The horse snorted nervously. "I swear, I'm going to have to shoot that goddamn horse. Look, Richard, I feel awful about this. That was a buck, wasn't it? Let me give you two hundred for him."

Delia held Xerxes at arm's length from her, staring. She screamed. Richard watched her.

"Richard?"

"What?"

"About the buck, I want to give you two hundred for him. Say, what's wrong? There wasn't anything special about him, was there?"

"No. No. Nothing."

Beneath the agony of Delia's face, Richard was fascinated by a strange and wild kind of beauty, something exquisitely revealed by her pain. He had found her desirable before, but never like this, with such terrible intensity.

"There *is* something the matter," Ned said.

"What? Oh. No. No."

"Let's go back to the house. You can draw up a bill of sale for two hundred."

"Bill of sale?"

Ned frowned. "For the buck, the suckler."

"That's ridiculous. It was hardly five months old, wouldn't have brought a penny on the market."

They led their horses away.

"Really," Ned said, "I do wish you'd let me pay you for it . . . ."

Richard was looking back over his shoulder at Delia.

In the evening, as the leavings from supper were being cleared under the direction of Sadie, who headed the kitchen staff, Richard said: "Oh, Sadie. I want you to add Delia, that wench with the reddish skin, to your crew. You can start her tomorrow."

"She ain't no house nigger," Sadie said scornfully. "She nothin' but a dirty *field* nigger. She doan belong here."

"Well, bring her here anyway," Richard said. "And don't get huffy about it."

Amanda stiffened at Delia's name. "That's all, Sadie. You can go now." She waited a moment, then said, "I don't think this is a good idea, Richard, bringing that wench into the house."

She dabbed at her lips with a napkin, waiting.

He sat back and lighted his pipe.

"Well?" she said.

"Well, what?"

"I just told you," she said coolly, "that I don't like bringing

Delia into the house. She's a contrary nigger. She's caused nothing but trouble in the past."

"Uh-hm."

"What are you going to do about it?"

"Do?" Richard took the pipe from his mouth and smiled. "Mother, now that I'm master of Olympus, I should exercise my own judgment, don't you think?"

JUD DID NOT LEARN of Xerxes' death until he returned from the fields that evening. He felt a sense of loss; he had been growing fond of the baby.

Delia wept bitterly and sat hunched in a corner. She would not let him come near her. His hands fumbled helplessly, and as he watched her struggle alone with her sorrow his anger grew.

Finally, when her tears began to abate, he moved to her side. He put his arm lightly around her. She didn't respond.

"Delia. Delia girl," he said into her hair.

"He gone, Jud. He crushed dead."

"I know. An' we both know he ain't goin' come back. But you still here, an' I still here."

"Why he gone? Why it have to be him?"

"There ain't no reason. There no reason for nothin'. It jus' is," he said roughly. "It jus' is."

"They kilt him!"

"Yes. An' he gone, Delia. You unnerstan'? Gone. But there goin' be more. There goin' be li'l sucklers twice as fat. They goin' be your sucklers." He tightened his grip around her. "We goin' care for 'em. We goin' watch ovuh 'em—on that mountain if 'n you want. You want that, Delia?"

She nodded slowly. "Yes. All alone." She turned her face up to his. "We goan have another suckler, Jud? Truly? An' we goan 'tect it ourse'ves?"

"Yes."

"Oh!" She buried her face against his chest and began to cry again.

They fell asleep together, she nestled closely to him, his heavy arms clasping her.

AFTER HER FIRST DAY in the kitchen of the Great House, Delia raged around the shanty.

"Who that black Sadie bitch think she is? That uppity nigger ack like I a rag to wipe her feet on. An' Mist'ess 'Manda. She got meanness fo' me. I see it in her eyes an' hear it when she talk." She flung a tin plate down from the shelf. "Hhhmph!"

Jud turned a piece of firewood over in his hands, toying with it; he flexed and loosened his muscles against it.

"Soon," he said. "We goin' to that mountain soon."

Delia looked at him, and apprehension crept into her eyes. "They . . . they won't cotch us, will they?"

"Maybe. I don' know."

Delia looked down at the floor.

"You 'fraid?" Jud asked.

She nodded.

"You want t' stay?"

She gnawed on her lip a moment, and shook her head. She was silent awhile; then she said, "Whut they do if they cotch us?"

Jud set down the wood. "We got to wait the right time. I

s'pose' to spen' a few days movin' roun' Mista Richard's othuh plantations, workin' wood. Then we pass a few more days, an' the firs' dark night we run. Soon. 'Fore plantin' season."

Delia turned away from him.

"Come here."

He took her hand as she approached and guided her down to the floor in front of him. She laid her head on his knee. He cupped her face with one hand and stroked her hair with the other.

RICHARD MADE NO ATTEMPT to restrain his mother or Sadie. They both resented Delia's presence in the house, and this resentment was expressed in savage verbal assaults upon the girl. And the more she was attacked, the haughtier and more aloof she grew. Richard held himself in check, not going near her, even though his impulse was to take her without further delay. He wanted her pride to climb to its highest summit.

Then he would break her.

Shortly before supper on the third day, Richard was brought springing to his feet in the sitting room by Amanda's scream.

"*Richard!*"

He ran down the hall and through the dining room, and into the kitchen.

Amanda was in the center of the room, next to a table on which rested platters of meat, a large steaming kettle, and a silver soup tureen. Her face was blanched, her small wide-set eyes were slitted, and she was trembling. Her cheek and dress were spattered with liquid.

Delia stood across the room, her back against the wall, brandishing a heavy soup ladle like a club. Sadie and two other wenches cowered in the far corner.

"What happened?"

Amanda raised her arm, pointing. "Her! That devil-bitch you brought into the house. She attacked me! Threw hot soup at me. At *me!*"

Richard was angry. The time was not right. He wasn't ready yet.

"Well, what did you do to her?" he demanded of Amanda.

She whirled and slapped him, sputtering furiously, unable to speak.

Richard recoiled, shocked back to reality. "Hector," he bellowed. "Hector, get in here."

The liveried butler appeared. "Take her to the barn and hold her until I get there," Richard said.

"Yes, suh."

Delia edged away as Hector approached, then bolted for the door. Hector grabbed her. She snarled and beat him about the head with the ladle. He knocked it from her hand. She kicked and clawed at him. He pinned her arms, then slung her small body over a hip and carried her out.

"Bitch!" Delia screamed at Amanda. "Bitch!"

"Richard," Amanda said. "I want you to hurt her. Do you understand? Hurt her."

Richard took her arm and led her back into the dining room. "Yes, Mother," he said.

After supper he went to the barn. He had two blacks strip the girl naked and hold her down on a bench. Delia said nothing. Her face was unrepentant. Richard took up a long, thin, supple rod he'd cut from a peach tree. He swished it through the air to test its spring. At the sound, Delia's buttocks tightened. Richard smiled. The moment was premature, but, he decided, by no means lost.

The first blow struck the girl just above her knees. After that, Richard worked the rod slowly and methodically up the length of her body. When the swollen red welts marked her from knees to neck, he returned to her buttocks and concentrated on them. The girl was whimpering and the slaves holding her exerted all their strength to keep her from jerking out of their grasp. Her hips and loins pounded against the bench as she tried to escape the rod.

She was crying out, and that was good, Richard thought, but there was no real subjugation in her voice, only an involuntary response to pain. Still, it was a beginning.

He laid into her buttocks with a frenzy. He was panting. His mouth opened. His accuracy began to fail. Then suddenly he dropped the rod, twisted to the side, clutched his groin with both hands, and gave a long, low moan.

When he straightened he said, "Have her washed down. That will be enough for now."

DELIA LAY FACE DOWN and unclothed atop the bed in her shanty. Jud had left early in the morning for Europa and had not yet returned; she was alone. Her skin was unbroken, but swollen and inflamed. She tried to force back the sobs, but they came anyway, twisting her on the bed in the darkness. She vacillated between them and snarling rage, clutching at the rough blanket and beating her small fists against the bed frame. Each time footsteps approached the shanty, she looked up hopefully, and began to edge herself painfully from the bed. But the footfalls were always those of someone passing by. At last a heavy tread did not veer off but came directly toward the door.

"Jud," Delia murmured. "Jud." Her cheeks grew wet again.

There was a knock on the door. Halfway off the bed, Delia stopped, suddenly afraid.

"Who there?" she said.

"Delia? It Chaskey." The door swung open, and the big foreman stood silhouetted in the moonlight.

"Whut you want, Chaskey?"

"Mista Richard want you up at the house. I s'pose' to bring you."

"Whut for?"

"I doan know. You best put a frock on. Cain't go like that."

"Chaskey? Whut he goan do?"

"I . . ." He let the sentence die. "We gots to hurry," he said gruffly. "Mista Richard doan like waitin.'"

Chaskey led her to the house and turned her over to a servant. Carrying a candle, the servant brought her up the back stairs, paused to look up and down the hall, and then hurried her to Richard's room and knocked softly.

"Come in."

The house black opened the door just wide enough to nudge Delia in, then hastily retired. Richard was standing at the foot of the bed, wearing a robe.

"Good evening," he said.

Delia stared at the wall. She stood at her full height, shoulders thrown back and head held high.

Richard locked the door and slipped the key into his pocket.

"Are you ignoring me?" he asked pleasantly. "Come now, look at me. Oh my, but that's a proud expression. Don't you know that, as it is said, 'Pride goeth before destruction'?"

He loosened the belt to his robe. The garment swung open. He was naked and excited beneath it. His voice dropped to a whisper.

"First," he said, "first I want you to get on your belly . . . and crawl to me . . . and lick my feet."

JUD RETURNED SEVERAL HOURS after nightfall. The moon was high and there were lights in only a few of the shanties. At first he thought Delia was asleep. He moved quietly to the bed, so as not to wake her, and reached out to touch her. The bed was empty.

"Delia?"

He struck flint and steel and lit the lamp. He looked around. Nothing seemed amiss. He went to the neighboring shanty. A frightened girl, anxious to close the door on him, told him that she knew nothing. When he persisted, threatening to force his way in, she said, "Chaskey. Go see Chaskey. He tell you."

Jud strode to Chaskey's shack and hammered on the door.

"Where Delia at?" he demanded when Chaskey answered.

The foreman looked down at his feet. Jud bunched his shirt in one hand and pulled him forward.

"Where is she!"

"Easy, Jud. I tell you."

Jud released him.

Chaskey rubbed the back of his neck. "Jud . . . Jud, they was trouble. Delia, she throw somethin' at Mist'ess 'Manda."

Jud stepped back as if struck.

"Mista Richard whup her. No," he said quickly, "not wif the snake. He take a rod to her. She pained, but she not bloodied."

Jud nodded. "Where is she now? With Emeral'?"

Chaskey looked away. "Uh . . . no. She, uh, she up at the house. Mista Richard send fo' her 'bout two hours ago."

"Whut for?"

"I doan know, Jud. I truly doan. But doan fret, they ain't goan cut her. You know they never bloody no nigger in the house."

Jud stood silent, breathing deeply. Then he turned to go.

"Jud!" Chaskey called. Jud stopped. "I . . . I . . ." The foreman could think of nothing to say. He lowered his head.

"Uh-huh," Jud said.

Jud went back to his shanty. He sat on a stool, leaning forward, elbows resting on his knees, hands clasped and supporting his head. In a while he stood, went to a corner, and picked up a frock Delia had been mending. He walked back to the stool. He sat, holding the frock, caressing it while the few remaining sounds from the slave quarters faded one by one.

He did not hear her enter; rather, suddenly became aware of her presence and looked up. She was standing in the doorway.

"Delia!" He leaped up and took her by the shoulders.

She seemed almost not to recognize him, to recognize that he was there at all.

He pulled her softly to him, careful not to touch her back. "Delia, it all right now. I here. It ovuh."

She stood still. Her arms hung at her sides.

"Delia?" He put a hand under her chin and raised her face so that she was looking into his eyes. Her own were blank. He took her hand. "Come," he said. She followed him to the bed and stood there until he guided her down.

When her buttocks touched the mattress, she gave a tiny cry. Jud helped her to lie down on her side. She neither helped nor resisted him.

"Delia, tell me whut wrong. Talk to me."

He tried for several minutes, but got no response. She seemed to be looking through him.

There were tears in his eyes. "Delia, please. Please talk to me. It me, Jud."

Her mouth opened. He took her face in his hands.

"I . . . I goan away." Her voice was distant. "I goan far away. Far . . . far. Goan away . . . an' nobody goan see Delia again . . . . I goan away."

Jud pressed his cheek to hers. "Yes, Delia. Soon. We goin' to that mountain." His voice was choked. "Soon. Jus' you an' me."

If she heard him, she offered no sign.

"Delia. Oh, Delia!" He pressed his face into her hair and wept.

After a while, he extinguished the lamp, sat down beside the bed, and leaned his back against the wall. He stroked Delia's hand and murmured, "Sleep. Sleep now."

In an hour his head began to nod.

HE WOKE A LITTLE before dawn with a start. The bed
was empty. The light seeping in the windows was a dark gray.
A quick glance around the shanty revealed everything in its
place, except Delia's worn pair of shoes, which usually stood
beside his own next to the door.

He touched the mattress. It was cold. She'd been gone for
some time.

He stepped outside. A thin arc of light was spread across
the eastern horizon. A handful of blacks were shuffling sleepily through the quarters. The boy assigned to beat the morning
tattoo on the iron triangle was trudging toward the meeting
shed, rubbing the sleep out of his eyes with his knuckles. Jud
went back inside and waited until the clanging triangle had
been silent for some minutes and there were many blacks up
and moving about. Then he left the shanty and sought out
the overseer.

"Suh," he said. "Delia burn all night with the fever. She
pow'ful weak, cain't get out of bed."

"Oh? Well, maybe I should go give her a look."

"If'n you want, suh. But I dose her good with quinine an'
the fever break this mornin'. She jus' now close her eyes. She
be fine, be right back to work tomorrow. But I thought you
want to know 'bout it."

"All right. Fine. You git on to work now, look in on her
this afternoon. If'n she ain't better by evenin', you come git
me, hear?"

"Yes, suh."

Jud worked hard and with careful concentration through
the day. He cut, he bored, he polished, he fitted iron tools
perfectly with new shafts. He was acutely aware of the grain

of the wood he handled, the rough texture of the unfinished pieces, the burning odor that rose as the saw warmed in the tight slots when he cut planks, the crunching of the chips beneath his feet. It was a good, productive day's work, and he remained in the shop after most of the others had been vacated.

When he finally left, shortly before suppertime, he took a roundabout way back to his shanty, one that brought him past the slaughterhouse. As he had expected, it was empty. Beneath the bone saws and cleavers there was a rack that held an assortment of thin boning knives used for skinning and for fine cutting. He withdrew three of them, turned them over in his hands, and replaced two. The one he kept was narrow and flat, with a five-inch blade. He stuck it in his waistband and covered the hilt with his shirt.

In his shanty he lighted the oil lamp. From beneath the rags in the raffia basket he withdrew several scraps of paper, a newspaper, a quill, and a packet of black dye. He went through the pieces of paper first, and selected one on which someone from the Great House had written, and then crossed out, the first paragraph of a letter. Half of the piece was empty. He folded it, ran his palm along the edge to sharpen the crease, opened it, and tore it carefully on the fold. He discarded the smaller portion, the one with the writing on it. He sprinkled some of the powdered dye into a dish and added water. He thought for some time, furrowing his brow. He took a smaller, dirtied piece of paper, dipped the quill into the dye, and laboriously wrote the first sentence. He spent the next hour in practice, changing words, searching the newspaper to check his spelling as best he could. When he finally felt that he could do no better, he copied what he had written onto the large piece of paper. He wrote:

April 1861

To All Interested. This is Xerxes from Alan Peals Plantation. Cloud Haven. Tennessee. He got til May to get to Charleston to work for my cousins Grain & Feed Store in Charleston. Plees let him work for food if he want.

with respect

Alan Peal. Esq.

Xerxes. Delia would have liked that. He read over his work and was satisfied. He folded the paper with care and tucked it into a bandana in which he had placed some pone and a chunk of smoked meat.

Then he put out the lamp and sat down in the darkness. He waited, thinking of nothing, until the slave quarters were wrapped in silence. Then he emerged cautiously from the shanty and made his way to the Great House, keeping to the shadows.

The night was still save for the chirring of tree frogs and the hum of nocturnal insects. He studied the house as he approached, searching for even the tiniest glimmer of light. There was none. He located the window he wanted. It was at the corner of the house, on the second floor. Below it, a rain barrel stood on the ground, half full. He took off his shoes and set them down next to the barrel. He placed the bandana next to them. Then he stood and listened, sorting out the sounds of the night.

No one was awake.

He removed his shirt, put it with his shoes and the

bandana. He drew the knife from his waistband and clamped it in his teeth, and shucked out of his pants. Naked, he looked up. Between the first and second stories was a narrow cornice, and spaced along the cornice were projecting corbels—mostly decorative, but strong enough to support his weight. He tested the rain barrel. It was solid, wouldn't tip. Bracing one hand against the wall for balance, he climbed up on the barrel and stood on the rim, straddling the mouth. He readjusted the knife between his teeth, reached up, grasped one of the corbels, tested it, and swung off the barrel, kicking a leg high and catching the next corbel in the crook of his knee. Slowly he worked himself up so that he stood erect, legs spread, one foot on each of the corbels. He moved carefully along the wall, and several minutes later was crouching beneath the window he wanted.

He reached his fingers over the sill and probed. The window was barely open, not enough room for him to work his fingers beneath it. He took the knife from his teeth and pressed the blade against the wall to test it. It gave slightly. It was not meant for heavy work, but he thought it would be stiff enough. He slipped it between the window and the sill, levered it slightly. He pressed harder. There was a small scrape, which made him go rigid, as the window edged up. He waited. When he heard nothing from within, he rose to his full height. Curtains masked the window, but the drapes were open, and Jud could see the outline of a bed and a sleeping figure.

He set the knife carefully on the sill and took hold of the frame with both hands. His vision did not waver from the bed as he inched the window up, paused, inched it up again, paused . . . .

The figure rolled twice, but didn't wake. Jud picked up the knife and lifted a leg over the sill and into the room. The carpet felt strange to his bare foot, curiously soft, and without the chill of the ground or of bare floors. He bent his torso low, swung beneath the window, and drew his other leg after him. He parted the curtains, and purposely left them parted so that moonlight spilled in.

He crossed the room, placing his feet carefully and feeling with his toes for obstructions. At the side of the bed he stood looking down at Richard Ackerly's sleeping form. The white man was lying on his side, his back to Jud. Jud crouched, took hold of a corner of the blanket and gave it a little tug. Richard grunted and pulled the blanket closer to his chin. Jud tugged again. A kind of sigh came from Richard. He rolled over onto his back.

Jud stood, grasped the knife, and leaped upon the white man, driving his knee deep into Richard's stomach, covering his mouth with one great hand. Richard's eyes bulged open. Air rushed warmly through his nostrils and his mouth tried to open beneath Jud's hand. His fists beat at Jud's head, his fingers clawed for the eyes.

"Quiet, Mista Richard," Jud whispered. He held the knife out so Richard could see it. "Quiet. Quiet."

Richard bucked and twisted under him, but Jud's weight was too great. Jud dimpled the side of Richard's neck with the point of the knife. The skin separated and a small drop of blood appeared.

"Quiet," Jud said. Richard ceased to struggle. He stared up through wide eyes. "Kin you see me, Mista Richard? Blink yo' eyes if you kin. Good. That's good. You rec'nize me? Jud, right? Good."

He looked down at Richard with an expressionless face. Then he laid the keen edge of the knife across Richard's throat.

"You feel that? Uh-huh. Well, you jus' rest a bit an' think 'bout it. Think 'bout how sharp it is. Think 'bout where it set-tin'. You thinkin' 'bout that, Mista Richard? Good."

Jud shifted his weight suddenly and brought it to bear on the knife, pressed the thin blade down through flesh and car-tilage, drawing it a little to the side. Richard's eyes distend-ed. He kicked out. He flailed at Jud. Blood spurted from his throat, spraying hot onto Jud's arms and chest. The knife pressed against the hard vertebrae of Richard's neck. Jud held it there, keeping his other hand over Richard's mouth. Richard thrashed about wildly, but without effect. Small wet cough-ing sounds issued from his gaping throat. Jud felt Richard's stomach convulse, and an instant later a thick liquid erupted over Jud's forearms. Richard's struggles grew weaker, but still the blood gushed over Jud, soaking the bedding, and still Jud did not relinquish his hold.

It was only when Richard had been motionless for several minutes that Jud eased back, then released him, moved off the bed. He glanced down at Richard, turned and walked to the window, leaving the knife wedged in Richard's throat. He climbed out through the window, steadied himself, and sprang lightly to the ground, rolling to absorb the shock.

He rested a moment and listened. When he heard noth-ing that was not natural to the night, he pushed himself up and padded silently to the rain barrel. He took hold of each side of the rim, flexed his arms, and drew up his legs. He lowered himself into the chilly water. Taking care not to splash, he squatted and worked his hands over his body and swirled the water about himself.

He emerged washed free of blood. He rolled his shirt into a ball, used it to wipe himself dry, and dressed quickly.

Once he had gained the public road, he stopped to put on his shoes. He looked up at the moon. Dawn was a little less than four hours away. A man walking leisurely can cover four miles in an hour. A man running steadily, running smoothly, can travel twice that distance.

Jud began to run.

When the first pink fingers of light splayed into the sky, he entered the woods. He stayed near the road, for the foliage was thinner there and would not slow him as much as the deeper woods. He didn't stop until the sun was well past meridian, and then only long enough to eat some pone. He had no difficulty avoiding the few travelers, white and black, whose paths he crossed. Toward sunset he slanted away from the road, farther into the woods. At the bank of a small stream he rested for a while, but did not allow himself to close his eyes. At dark he was off again, back on the roads. It was easier on them, much easier, and he knew, when he reentered the woods an hour before dawn, that he would have to travel on them during the day, too. Fighting through the undergrowth was difficult, and he couldn't cover enough ground. Staggering with weariness, he threw himself down in a clearing. He lay only a moment, though, for there were things he had to do before he could sleep. He scraped up a pile of dust, then stripped off his shirt, pulled up his pants legs, and rubbed the dust vigorously onto his skin, working it into his pores. It wasn't much, but it helped, lightening the deep hue of his color. Then he searched for two stones, a short one with a narrow blunt point, and a second, round, heavy one. He rolled back his upper lip and placed the blunt stone against his teeth. It was a good width; it covered the two center teeth. He held the stone steady, picked up the second one, and used it to strike the first, as he would have used a hammer to strike a chisel. He groaned as the two teeth snapped off at the gum line. He spat them out, along with viscous, saliva-mixed blood. He took green moss from the side of a tree and held it against his injured gums until it stuck. Then he crawled under a thick bush, so the sun would not shine on him when it rose, and fell immediately into a deep and exhausted slumber.

He woke in the late afternoon. He removed the moss and tested the gums. The bleeding had stopped. He walked back to the road, but before leaving the woods, he picked up a knobby-ended stick, the length of a cane. There were not many travelers. When they did approach, Jud stooped and affected a limp. No one paid any unusual attention to him.

Toward the end of the day, he came upon a roadside inn. There was a small coffle—five chained blacks and a white man—preparing to bed down for the night. Two gentlemen sat in rockers on the porch, and another, a traveler from the look of his clothes, was watering his horse. A black man was scooping water from the horse trough with his hand. Leaning against the trough was a stick with a red-and-yellow tote sack tied to the end.

Jud approached them, limping slightly, enough to be noticed, but not enough to draw undue notice.

"Evenin', Masta. Evenin' to you, suh," he said to the man
watering his horse. He grinned and bobbed his head. "Kin
you tell me, Masta, suh, how far I gots to go 'fore I gets me to
Charleston?"

The white man looked up, then returned his attention to
his horse. "You got a goodly walk yet, nigger. Better'n a hunnert an' fifty miles."

"Oooh-eee! Thank you, suh. Thank you, Masta." The
white man turned his horse away, started to lead it off, then
stopped. He squinted at Jud. "Whut your name, nigger?"

Jud smiled broadly and puffed out his chest. "Xerxes, suh."

"Mmm-hmm. Lemme see your pass."

"Yes, suh. It right here, suh."

The man took the paper and silently mouthed the words
as he read it. He finished, scratched his upper lip, and handed the pass back. "Well, if'n you goin' team up with another
walkin' nigger, you better be right careful."

Hoofbeats pounded down the road, and above them came
a shout, "Ai-yah-ai-yah-hoo!"

"They somethin' dangery, suh?"

The man was watching the rapidly approaching rider with
curiosity.

"Suh?"

"Whut? Oh, a lunatic buck—a big bastard—an' his wench.
Went mad upstate an' kilt a white man. Headin' north, most
likely, but you never can tell with crazy niggers. Though they
wouldn't o' got this far if they movin' south, anyway."

Jud shuddered. "Lordy! Thank you, Masta. Thank you, suh."

The rider, a young man with a flushed face, forced his galloping mount into a sharp turn which nearly caused them both to spill. He raced the lathered animal into the yard—"*War!*"—and jerked it to a vicious stop.

The men on the porch were standing. "Whut you sayin', boy?"

"War!" The boy leaped from the saddle and ran up to them. "They's gonna be a war!"

"Now calm down. Whut kind of foolishness you talkin'?"

"Goddamn it, ain't no foolishness! It God's gospel truth. We damn near blowed Fort Sumtuh into kingdom come wif our cannon. The Yankees run up the white flag."

"Where'd you hear that?"

"Courier jus' ride hell-bent into town. We goin' to war! An' that ain't all. The Yanks gonna use niggers to fight. They givin' all them niggers up Norf guns an' uny-forms, goin' send 'em agin' us! *Niggers!*"

"No!"

"Not even the Yanks'd do that!"

When his departure would no longer seem conspicuous, Jud limped away from the inn. The stars were already bright in the sky above him. He walked slowly, and for a little while the voices from the inn followed him.

Then he was alone.

Maybe the Quakers could help him find Delia. If they couldn't, or if she was . . . If they couldn't . . .

He stopped and looked up. Not at the stars, but at the huge emptiness that separated him from them.

If they couldn't . . . Maybe he would go to Canada. Maybe he would go North and see if they would make a soldier of him. Maybe he would go and find the mountain. Maybe—

He didn't know what he would do. He was free.

He didn't know what that meant.

Jerrold Mundis is the author of more than a dozen novels, half a dozen of books of nonfiction, and a number of ghostwritten books. His books have been selected by the Book-of-the-Month Club, the Literary Guild, the One Spirit Book Club, and other book clubs, and translated into more than a dozen foreign languages. His short work has appeared in publications ranging from the *New York Times Magazine* and *American Heritage* to the *Magazine of Fantasy & Science Fiction*. He is an experienced literary coach and teacher of professional and avocational writing. He lives in New York City.

Contact Jerrold Mundis

Email: jerry@jerroldmundis.com
Blog: jerroldmundis.com/blog
Facebook: www.facebook.com/jerrold.mundis
Website: www.jerroldmundis.com
Twitter: @JerroldMundis

NEWSLETTER: Jerrold Mundis sends out a newsletter from time to time with updates, announcements, and special offers. It's free—and all you have to do to get on the list is send an email to jm@jerroldmundis.com with the word NEWSLETTER in the subject box. That'll do it.

Your email address will never be shared, you won't get any spam, and you can unsubscribe at any time with a single click.

THE SHAME & GLORY SAGA

Slave Ship: Book I

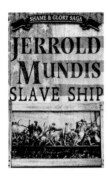

A major novel of the American slave trade that annihilates the myths of black African docility and white humanity on an unforgettable nightmare voyage that takes the reader into the hearts and minds and private hells of the slavers as well as the enslaved.

Slave: Book II

A raw and unbridled novel of slavery in the Deep South.

Shattered by the forces of unrest and upheaval that preceded the Civil War, the Ackerly Plantation is caught up in a frenzy of violence, cruelty, and hatred.

Here is the brutal reality of slavery—of men and women sold at auction—of young girls forced to gratify their master's lust—of slaves tortured until their only remaining instinct is to strike back . . . to kill.

The Long Tattoo: Book III

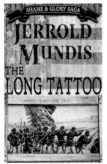

A brutal saga of the Civil War—and a regiment of fugitive slaves that thirsted for revenge. Scarred, branded, unchained, they were the First Southern Volunteers, a Union regiment of fugitive slaves suddenly armed and free to avenge a lifetime of pain and degradation—some with a savagery that knew no bounds and offered no mercy.

Hellbottom: Book IV

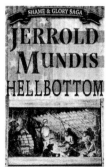

A savagely real novel of degradation, violence and slaves without chains.

They were the hunted, the outcasts, the men who had fired guns too quickly and the woman who had been raped too often. There was no place for them in the white world. They were free black men and women driven to a womb of hell by incredible brutality—and their only salvation lay in the merciless justice of the swamp itself. They became hard, wary, their eyes caught the smallest movements, their ears the slightest sounds. The swamp punished even the most simple mistakes with death, so they, like all other creatures in Hellbottom, were the finest of their kind. They were ruthless, deadly and waiting . . . and one day the hunters came.

Running Dogs: Book V

A hard, unflinching novel of men—black and white—locked in a struggle against themselves, each other, and the unforgiving landscape of the American West.

There is only so much a man can take, and the men of the Second Colored Cavalry had taken enough. So in spit-shine dress uniforms, on the regiment's finest horses, a group of them rode into the town of Roxbury Run, tied their mounts to the hitching rail, and walked into the Dead Ringer Saloon . . . .

Where they were not wanted.

Printed in Great Britain
by Amazon